Look for the other books in the

Book of Signs

John Peel

AN
APPLE
PAPERBACK

SCHOLASTIC INC.
New York Toronto London Auckland Sydney

Cover art by Michael Evans

ISBN 0-590-05948-3

12 11 10 9 8 7 6 5 4   7 8 9/9 0 1 2/0

Printed in the U.S.A.

First Scholastic printing, August 1997

This is for
Howard and Debbie Margolin

PROLOGUE

"So, they've managed to kill Aranak." The Wizard looked up from her scrying pool at her familiar. He was, as usual, perched on his little padded tower, and apparently asleep. "They're more dangerous than I thought." Winding a strand of hair around her finger thoughtfully, she added: "It might help if you actually woke up and did some work for a change."

The red panda opened one eye and regarded her for a moment. "I *am* awake," he answered, with a yawn. He rearranged his long, fluffy tail and closed his eye again. "I just haven't been paying attention."

The Wizard snorted. Blink and she had a stormy relationship at best. She, the Wizard Shanara, was a whirlwind of activity. Blink spent ninety-five percent of his time sleeping or trying to sleep. "Well, pay attention," she snapped. "Those three youngsters have killed Aranak, and they may be after me next. In which case, you'd starve."

With a sigh, Blink opened both eyes. Heaving himself reluctantly into a seated position, he started to groom himself. "Very well," he answered, as if she'd just condemned an innocent man to death. "Tell me about it."

Shanara counted to ten to keep her temper. If she didn't need Blink's help, she had plenty of ideas on what to do with him. Most of them meant he wouldn't live very long. "There are three youngsters," she said. "There's one named Score. He's some kind of street urchin from Earth. There's one called Renald, from a world called Ordin. She's disguised herself as a boy, which fools some people, but not me. And the last one's Pixel, from Calomir. The three of them were taken by the Beastials to Treen. There they were taught magic by Aranak. In a showdown, they managed to defeat and kill him before coming through the Portal that leads them *here*. They're now on Rawn. I've been observing them in my scrying pool for the past hour while you slept. They have the Pages that they discovered, and they may even know that I have one more. At any rate, it looks like they're going to be on their way here."

"Oh, dear," Blink muttered. "That sounds too much like work to me."

"Yes," she agreed. "That's just what it is. We have to slow them down, and give me a chance to come up with a plan to defeat them."

"Where are they?" asked Blink.

"In the Jagged Mountains," Shanara answered, studying their images in her pool.

"Well, then, you probably don't have to bother worrying about them," the panda answered. "Considering what's in there with them."

"They're more powerful than they look," the Wizard commented. "I'd be a fool to rely on the dangers on those mountains alone to stop them. No, I'm going to have to take an active hand in this one."

"Ouch," muttered Blink. "And I *know* that means work."

"Yes," Shanara agreed. "But it will eliminate a potential threat. If the mountains don't get those kids, then we shall." With a faint smile, she returned to studying her pool. Blink sighed again and wondered about his chances of catching forty more winks before he actually had to — shudder! — *work.* . . .

CHAPTER 1

Score stared all around, alternately fascinated and appalled. He, Renald — no, *Helaine*! — he had to get used to her being female — and Pixel had emerged from the Portal ready, they had thought, for anything. Mostly, they had expected to be either attacked or captured. Instead, there was nobody waiting for them at all.

And they had emerged on the edge of a precipice.

All around them were mountains shaped like jagged teeth. They were obviously high up, with a very chill wind whipping about them, as if trying to push them over the edge. Score swallowed hard. He was a

1

city boy, born and raised in New York. He wasn't used to wilderness, and he certainly wasn't used to mountains. And he *hated* being stuck on the side of one.

Behind them was a blink of light, but it was just the Portal closing down, its job done.

"Well," Score said heavily. "That's it. We're stuck here now."

"I don't like it," Pixel admitted, stepping back slightly from the edge of the drop. "It looks dangerous. What do you think, Renald?"

"It *is* dangerous," Helaine said, a little of her old temper showing through. She seemed to have grown to like Score and Pixel a little, but she was still impatient with them from time to time. Score supposed it came from being brought up as a spoiled daughter of a wealthy Lord and also as a warrior. She was the only one of the three who could fight properly, and this had a tendency to make her arrogant and short-tempered. She was, however, trying to control it. "And call me Helaine, please. I prefer my real name, now that you know who I am."

"Well, I prefer my street name," Score commented, shivering. "It's cold, and I'm not dressed for mountaineering."

"None of us are," Pixel agreed, his teeth starting to chatter. "We'd better get out of this wind and make plans."

Score glanced around, trying not to get sick when he saw how precarious their perch was. Above them, low clouds clung to the peak of the mountain, obscuring the view. He gestured down the narrow path they were standing on. "There's a cave down there," he said. "Let's get inside it. Then we can whip up a fire to get warm."

"Good idea," Helaine conceded. She moved past him to lead the way down. Score was about to object, but decided not to. It wasn't worth fighting over. And if anyone fell, it would be her and not him. Cautiously, they all followed the narrow path down the side of the mountain. Finally, they all tumbled into the small cave he'd seen.

It was about ten feet deep and, after a narrow entrance where they had to stoop, it was about eight feet tall. It was also, thankfully, empty of other life. Once inside, the bitter chill of the wind was gone. It was still very cold, though.

Score concentrated on a loose rock on the floor. He visualized a flame in his mind, one that would warm them up, and heat the rock through. Then he focused this on the rock. "Shriker Kula prior," he murmured, using the incantation to create fire.

A sheet of flame leaped up, almost singeing Helaine. With a curse, she stumbled back. "That wasn't funny!" she snapped.

"I wasn't trying anything," Score protested, amazed. The flame died down a little, but burned brightly and warmly in the small cave. "I was just trying to start a small fire. Not a volcano."

"It's because we've crossed from the Outer Worlds to the Middle Circuit," Pixel said quickly. "Remember what Aranak told us? That the closer we get to the center of the Diadem, the stronger the magic grows? Obviously, a spell that would cause a small fire on Treen can cause a larger one here."

Helaine studied the flames thoughtfully. "And probably a forest fire if we get any closer to the center of the web of worlds," she suggested. "We're going to have to be very careful about using our powers here, until we can be sure we know what effect they'll have."

"*If* we can tell what effect they'll have," Score pointed out. "Don't forget, something is messing up the source of magic, and sending spells all wrong."

"I'm not forgetting," Helaine answered. "But since it's unpredictable, we just have to deal with it as it happens." She warmed her hands at the fire. "Well, I'm feeling better now. It might be an idea to take stock of what we've got, and see how much sense we can make of it. Let's pool our resources."

Score glared at her. "Will you stop always taking

4

command?" he complained. "I think we should *vote* for a leader, not just allow you to take over the role."

Helaine snorted. "And we'd all vote for ourselves," she pointed out. "That's a dumb suggestion. Look, I'm just the best person for the job. I'm used to giving orders and making plans."

"So?" Score snapped back. "Just because you were a royal pain in the butt on your world doesn't mean a thing here. I'm really bad at taking orders, especially from a girl."

She moved her hand to the hilt of her weapon. "A girl with a sword," she said softly.

"Hold it, guys!" protested Pixel, moving between them. "Arguing like this isn't going to get us anywhere. We've got to learn to work together, remember? That's what Oracle told us."

Score took a deep breath. "You're right," he agreed reluctantly. "We won't solve anything behaving like this." Then he scowled again. "But I still say we have no reason to trust Oracle. He *claims* to be helping us, but he's sure managed to get us into a lot of trouble." The mysterious, flickering character had betrayed Score to a street gang on Earth, and the other two on their worlds also. He claimed to be on their side, but spent all his time spouting silly rhymes and avoiding giving them direct answers to any questions.

Pixel nodded. "I'm not sure I trust him, either," he admitted. "But he *may* be able to help us here. Surely it can't hurt to ask him?"

"I don't know," Helaine said. "He gives me a headache." Then she shrugged. "But we do need to know where we are, and what we should do here. And if there's anything to watch out for. I guess calling him up and asking him can't hurt that much."

"Right." Score decided it was time for him to take command, before Helaine could do it again. "We know we can call him up by focusing on his name and image. And then reciting his name backward for the calling spell. Together, then." He closed his eyes and concentrated. Oracle . . . in his pure black costume . . .

"I hear your call and I obey
To see what you require today."

Score opened his eyes, and there was Oracle, standing opposite them, a wide grin on his handsome face, and spouting his silly verses again. He claimed he had no option but to speak like that. Score wondered if he was telling the truth, or doing it just to irritate them. "I'll tell you what we require," Score growled. "Information. Where *are* we? What's going

on? And how do we get down off this stupid mountain?"

Oracle glanced around, and then stooped to peer
out of the cave. His lips quirked again with a smile.

"A raging wind, a fearful blast
Could tear you down from here quite fast."

He gestured with his hand, indicating someone
dropping over the edge like a rock.

"This world is known as Rawn, young friends,
Delightful, once the mountain ends.
But humans are not welcomed here
And danger to you soon will steer."

"Well, like I needed to hear *that*," complained
Score. "Danger. Why am I not surprised?"

"What kind of danger?" asked Helaine, rather
more practically.

"At mountain's base the goblin race
Assert their rule upon this place."

"Goblins?" echoed Pixel. "Marvelous. Goblins!
And nasty ones, too." He sighed. "So, we can't stay

here, or we'll freeze and starve to death. But if we go down the mountain, there's a band of goblins that will attack us." He eyed Oracle with outright anger. "Do you have *any* good news for us at all?"

Oracle shrugged.

"The news I give is true, not made,
But at least you have me for an aid."

Helaine snorted. "Why doesn't that make me feel any better?" she asked. Turning to Pixel and Score, she said, "Right, it's time to take stock of what we've got from Treen. Empty your pockets."

A few moments later, they had a very small pile indeed. There was Aranak's book of spells, which they hadn't yet had a chance to examine. There was the loose Page that Score had brought from Earth, and the one they had found in Aranak's study that seemed to be written in either some unknown language or code, which they couldn't read.

"Another page you soon will find
If you keep the crown in mind."

Oracle's comment was useful to consider, in good time. Right now, they continued with their inventory. The last item was a small pouch that the Beastials had given them. Helaine picked it up, undid the strings, and emptied the contents onto the ground in front of them.

They all stared in amazement. Glittering in the light from the flames were three almost impossibly large gemstones. There was a large ruby, as red as blood; an emerald, greener than any meadow in the spring; and a sapphire so blue it put the sky to shame.

Score's fingers twitched, and he reached out for the emerald, which seemed to be calling to him. He remembered the dreams he'd been having, and the giant gemstone that had seemed to speak to him. "This must be worth a fortune," he breathed, thinking how much it might fetch if sold to the right person in New York. But that was just a reflex, a shadow of the old Score speaking. He *knew*, somehow, that this was more than just a precious stone. It felt as if there was a gem-shaped hole in his soul into which this happened to fit perfectly.

"More than that," Helaine replied, reverently picking up the sapphire and cupping it in her hands. For once, she seemed to be overcome by an emotion that wasn't anger.

"Yeah," was all Pixel could manage as his hands gingerly clasped the ruby and brought it up to where he could study the dancing reflections of firelight within the gem. This made Score glance at the emerald. He remembered the greenish light of his dreams. Could they somehow be connected?

"I can hear a noise," Pixel said suddenly. "It sounds as if it's coming from *inside* the wall over there."

"Inside?" Helaine frowned. "But that's stupid. How could anything be *inside* solid rock?" She turned to ask Oracle a question, then sighed in exasperation. "He's gone again."

"Figures," Score muttered. He tried concentrating on the rock wall ahead of them, and gingerly reached out to touch it. There was a dull shaking that ran through his fingertips. "Hey!" he exclaimed. "There *is* something going on here! I can feel some sort of vibration."

"Stand back," Helaine ordered, drawing her sword. "Oracle's right — I can feel some kind of attack on its way. I'm the best to face it first."

Though her tone irritated Score, he managed to force his anger down. She was right, of course. She was certainly the better fighter. But he was more powerful when it came to magic.

A moment later, there was a loud cracking sound and the entire back wall of the cave exploded outward. Flying chips and lumps of rock sent the three companions reeling, as they tried to protect their faces. Dust in the air made Score cough, and he couldn't see anything for several seconds.

But he could hear. There was a loud, raucous chorus of jubilant voices, all of them squeaky and grating. "We did it!" "Ha! There they are!" And: "Get 'em, lads! Now!"

Out of the hole in the wall poured a wave of what had to be goblins.

CHAPTER 2

Helaine, coughing and choking from the dust, staggered back from the newly formed tunnel, trying to protect her face from chips of flying rock, and to retain her grip on her sword. Blinking, she managed to clear her eyes, even with tears streaming down her cheeks. In the entrance of the hole were several small, warped creatures. In the flickering of the flames from Score's fire, shadows were cast across the cave, making it hard to be certain what she was seeing.

Later, she managed to sort out her impressions, but then all she could see was that they were all about four feet tall, perfectly proportioned, but *twisted*. Their faces were like dried prunes, with large noses, mouths that were gashes filled with crooked teeth, ears that were pointed and hairy, and hands that were wrinkled but strong-looking. They were all dressed in tunics and pants, with heavy boots on the feet. And they all had short, untidily cropped shaggy hair that was filled with dust and grime.

And all of them were armed with pickaxes, staves, or thick knives, which they waved about as they swarmed out to the attack.

Helaine felt a moment's panic — not for herself, because these goblins seemed to lack discipline or leadership — but for Score and Pixel. Neither boy was armed. Which meant it was all up to her.

With a roar of rage, she threw herself forward, swinging her sword in as wide a circle as she could within the confines of the cave. Several of the goblins shrieked and backed off. This put them right in the path of their companions still pushing forward. About a dozen of them went down in a heap, cursing, yelping, and struggling. Several of them started hitting their companions as they struggled to get to their feet. Helaine blinked in amazement. The goblins seemed to be as happy fighting one another as they were fighting the three humans!

Then six of them managed to work their way around the struggling mass and jumped for the humans. Helaine stayed firmly in their way, knowing she could kill the goblins almost with ease if she wanted to. But she didn't want to. True, they had attacked first, without warning, but they weren't exactly brilliant fighters. It wouldn't be a battle to kill them — it would be butchery.

And Helaine had only ever killed one person in her life, and that had been Aranak. In that case, she had had no other choice. If she hadn't killed him, he would have killed the three of them. She still hadn't sorted out all of her emotions about being forced to kill another human being, but she knew that she didn't want any more blood on her hands than she was forced to take. With this decision made, she set about disarming the goblins and taking them out without too great an injury to any of them. Of course, if they started to get past her and attack Score and Pixel, she might be forced to change her mind.

The first goblin came at her, pickaxe raised, and screaming what was obviously some kind of war cry. Helaine swung carefully, neatly lopping the head off the weapon. The goblin looked confused for a second, and then continued, using the broken handle as a club. Helaine twisted out of the path of the blow, and backhanded him with the hilt of her sword. The goblin's eyes crossed, and then closed as he collapsed. A second goblin almost ran her through with his pickaxe. If

14

it wasn't for her magical ability to sense an attack before it happened, she would have been dead. As it was,
the blade clinked into the rock of the cave wall behind
her, and she managed to hit her attacker with the side
of her blade with enough force to send him tumbling
to join his unconscious friend on the cave floor.

Then three at once came at her, armed with
pikes. These were more cautious, intending to try and
spear her from a distance and not allow her to get in
too close to them with her sword. It was a smart
move, but didn't do them that much good. They poked
at her with enthusiasm, but kept getting in each
other's way in their eagerness to be the one to kill
her. Helaine simply grabbed the head of the pike closest to her, and pushed it to the right as hard as she
could. The goblin wielding it lost his footing and stumbled into the other two. All three went down in a bun-
dle, and they started punching and biting each other
as they struggled to regain their feet.

Pixel grabbed up one of the pikes the goblins had
dropped, and started to use it like a quarterstaff,
smacking any creature that came near him with the
wooden end of the stick. Helaine was slightly surprised to see that Pixel was actually quite good with
this method of fighting.

"Virtual Reality pays off sometimes," he told her.
"I always liked playing Robin Hood."

She had no idea what he was talking about, but as long as he wasn't helpless she felt slightly better. There was less pressure on her now, having only herself and Score to defend. She knew better than to expect him to be able to fight. He preferred running away from trouble. As she took on another couple of irate goblins, she spared a glance through the gloom to see what Score was actually doing.

She was so surprised that she almost let one goblin get too close. Score wasn't getting too close to the fighting — that part of his nature hadn't changed — but he'd evolved a way to help out. He was using his magical power to conjure up balls of fire, and was pitching them at the goblins. Screaming and panicking, the goblins ran around, trying to put out the flames. This mostly managed to get them into the paths of other attacking goblins, and they would inevitably end up in a tangled mass of arms, legs, and loud curses.

The goblins were definitely the noisiest and least disciplined fighters she'd ever faced. It wasn't hard to pick off one after another, either smacking them with the hilt of her sword, or with the flat of the blade, or simply just kicking them in their potbellied stomachs. She didn't even have to knock them out, because if any of her victims slammed into another goblin, the two creatures would forget about her and start in on each other instead. They obviously simply liked to fight, and didn't really care who they were attacking.

The problem was that there were just so many goblins that she was getting tired. Sooner or later, if the attack kept up, she was going to get exhausted. Pixel was doing pretty well with his pike, but he was skinny and not used to a lot of exercise. Helaine could see that he was tiring faster than she was. As for Score — doing magic was draining, too, so he wouldn't be able to keep up his barrage of fiery missiles for a whole lot longer.

Despite Score's fires, it was hard to see in the darkness. And she was finding it hard to keep her footing, because there were so many unconscious goblins on the floor of the cave now. She tripped over one, and almost fell onto a pike another was prodding in her direction. Then the goblin she had tripped over grabbed her ankle, and tried to knock her off her feet. He'd only been pretending to be unconscious, to lure her closer! Cursing herself for falling for the trick, Helaine struggled to stay upright, and to fend off the pike that was getting dangerously close to her face. She stomped down with her free foot on the goblin's hand, and he howled in pain. But he didn't let go, and struggled again to trip her up.

She whipped her sword around in an arc, shearing the tip off the pike. While her attacker stared at his shortened weapon in shock, Helaine slammed her sword down on the goblin's hand around her foot. The hilt must really have hurt the goblin, because he screamed, released her, and then jumped away, waving his hand and cursing loudly. He crashed into two other goblins, and they ended up brawling amongst themselves, as always.

Helaine retreated slightly, panting, and with sweat pouring down her face and back. "We can't keep this up much longer," she gasped to her companions.

"I can't," Pixel agreed. He was even sweatier than she was, and his hands were shaking from the strain. "We have to get rid of them somehow."

"No sweat," Score said, rather arrogantly. He grinned. He was the only one of them who didn't yet seem exhausted, but he was certainly showing the strain of all his magical spells. "Notice how big their eyes are?" he asked. "They're used to living underground."

"So?" snapped Helaine, back-handing another attacker, and sending him sprawling.

"So," Score said smugly, "both of you close your eyes . . . NOW!"

Helaine, though she had no idea what was happening, did as she was told. Even through her closed eyelids, she could see a huge flare of light, as Score cast another spell.

The conscious goblins all screamed, and then she could hear them stumbling away. She opened her eyes, blinking, to get rid of the yellow afterimage of the light, and could just see that all the goblins still erect were beating a very hasty retreat, slamming into the tunnel walls as they went.

"Just as I thought," Score announced. "They're used to darkness. So I just created a huge burst of light. It both blinded and hurt them. They won't be able to see a thing for hours."

Helaine stared at him, irritated by his smugness. But she forced herself to be fair. "That was good thinking," she said grudgingly. "They can't fight us if they're blind, so we're safe enough for now."

"We're more than safe," Pixel said, excitedly. He gestured at the tunnel. "It slopes downward. We can take it down to the base of the mountain, and avoid having to go down through the freezing snow outside. It should be a lot safer."

"There's likely to be a whole maze of tunnels down there," Score objected. "I don't like the idea of trying to find our way through it."

"We can always take one of the goblins prisoner if we have to," Helaine suggested, "and force him to show us the way out." Then she raised an eyebrow. "Or you could, of course, try the cold route down." She gestured at the mouth of the cave.

Score took one look outside and shivered. "No thanks," he decided. "I think I'll go for the less scenic route this time."

"Smart move," Pixel agreed. He shouldered his captured pike. "Well — shall we go?" He took the lead, stepping over fallen goblins, and started down the passageway ahead of them. Helaine shrugged and fell in behind him. Still muttering under his breath, Score brought up the rear.

What was waiting for them in the heart of the mountain?

"Well," said Blink, yawning widely and examining his claws, "that didn't go too well, did it? When's dinner? I'm starving."

Shanara straightened up from her scrying pool angrily. "Stop thinking about your stomach," she snapped. "Those children are more trouble than I anticipated. They've totally demoralized the goblins. Those little monsters won't attack them again."

"Not only that," Blink said, obviously enjoying goading her, "but they've even unwittingly provided the brats with a convenient way down the mountain. Now you can't even simply call up a wind and blow them over the edge of a cliff. Which," he added insultingly, "was *my* suggestion that you overrode. You had to go and get all creative and have the goblins involved."

The Wizard turned to her familiar with an overly sweet smile. "You asked about dinner," she purred. "How would you like to *be* dinner?"

"Cranky this morning, aren't we?" Blink replied. "You know very well you'd never eat me. You're on a diet, and, as you point out, I'm way too fat."

"Enough of that." Shanara stared back at her pool, thinking hard. "Well, if the goblins won't face intruders again, I'll have to find someone who will." She crossed to her desk, which was littered with scrolls. Sifting through them, she pulled open a map. "Here we are," she mused, examining it. "Ah! There's a small settlement of trolls quite close to the foot of the mountain. And trolls won't be anywhere near as simple for the three meddlers to defeat as the goblins were."

"Heigh–ho," muttered Blink, stretching. "*More* work . . ."

CHAPTER 3

The troll village was actually little more than a collection of neighboring caves, all with wooden steps leading to them, with doors, storage rooms and such added on. It had a very primitive air about it, because the trolls didn't want anything better. As long as they had a place to sleep, and somewhere to store their food and their few possessions, they were relatively happy. The average troll was about six and a half feet tall, and weighed over three hundred pounds. They were powerful and muscular, used to long bouts of endurance. Still, as long as they were left alone, the trolls were pretty much inclined to leave everyone else alone. When they weren't out hunting or cooking their catches, they spent as much time as possible simply lazing about. As a result, when the attack came, virtually all of the trolls in the village were there to witness it.

Tarkim had been dozing in the shade beside his cave when something roused him. Batting at the flies that always seemed to be hanging about, Tarkim yawned, stretched, and glanced down the trail to the forest. Then he stiffened in surprise.

There were three strangers there, looking at the village. And not simply strangers, but *humans*. Tarkim knew how rare this was, because humans were not welcome on Rawn. Most were killed as soon as any intelligent species spotted them. The only ones who survived were the stronger magic-users. And they tended to live in some out-of-the-way place and avoid contact with the natives of the planet.

Which meant that this trio had to be recent arrivals. Certainly nobody who had been on Rawn more than a few days would even think about approaching a troll village. Tarkim stretched again and started to clamber to his feet. It was about time he woke up his neighbors and they showed these intruders the error of their ways. Then he'd make sure they received a decent burial. Trolls weren't savages, after all, and it was only polite to bury your victims.

Before Tarkim could open his mouth and yell, the

three humans stepped out of the woods. Tarkim was puzzled. Why weren't they running? Not that it would do them much good, of course, since the trolls could outrace a fleeing deer, but they weren't exactly very intelligent humans. Then Tarkim realized why. From their size, they were just children, and they were obviously not very bright.

Well, they wouldn't live to grow any taller. Tarkim yelled an alarm, and all around him the other trolls started to grunt, scratch, and wake up.

Oddly, the three children didn't seem worried. Instead, they simply raised their arms, pointing both hands at the troll village. They seemed to be speaking something, but Tarkim couldn't hear anything at this distance.

Suddenly, fire shot from their outstretched fingers, leaping across the clearing and falling from the sky on the village.

Instantly, the wooden fabrications around the caves caught fire, and started to crackle and blaze. Tarkim bellowed, partly in surprise and partly in anger, before leaping to his feet. The three children seemed to be happy with their act of destruction, grinning at one another, and then turning back and vanishing into the forest.

Tarkim's own steps were ablaze, and he was

forced to leap over the flames to get clear. Hairs on the backs of his legs caught fire, and he batted out the flames, growling angrily. His steps cracked, splintered, and collapsed in a wall of flame that ignited his storehouse. All his stored meat was being burned to cinders! All his hunting, all his work, being destroyed in seconds!

And not only his! All around him, Tarkim's neighbors were howling in fury as they were forced to stand and watch their village go up in bright, burning flames and thick, choking smoke. The scent of burned meat filled the whole valley, as their stores were consumed.

"I saw the culprits!" Tarkim yelled loudly. He gestured toward the forest. "They ran off in that direction. We can soon catch them."

"Yes," growled one of his neighbor's wives, wringing her hands in fury. "And when we catch them, we grind their bones into dust! They'll pay for this!"

Turning their backs on their rapidly blazing village, the trolls started out as a group toward the trees. No matter how fast or how far those youths fled, they could never outrun a single troll — let alone the small army that was now on their track!

Exhausted, Blink flopped down again onto his cushion. "Why do your plans always involve so much work for me?" he complained. "And you still haven't said when dinner is. You're trying to starve me to death, aren't you? I'm wasting away."

Shanara snorted scornfully. "If you didn't eat for a year, it wouldn't hurt you," she replied. "You could live off your body fat." She stared again at her scrying pool. "That was a very effective illusion," she said admiringly. "I'd never have been able to fool the trolls like that without your help." In her pool, she could see the village — completely intact, in fact. The whole event that the trolls believed they had witnessed was nothing more than her elaborate illusion, coupled with the power of Blink. All of the trolls were absolutely convinced they had seen Score, Pixel, and Renald burn down their village.

"Well, let's hope *this* plan of yours works," Blink complained. "I can't take much more work like this without a good long rest. And a good long meal," he added, pointedly.

Ignoring his complaints, Shanara smiled. "Our three intruders are going to be in for a very nasty shock shortly."

Pixel groaned as they came to another fork in the tunnels. They had been traveling for several hours, going mostly downward. They hadn't seen any goblins at all, though they had heard small bodies moving around in the darkness. Score had conjured up a magic light that followed them like an eager puppy, and its light showed the trio their way ahead. It also kept the goblins from coming any closer. They really didn't like bright light at all.

The tunnels were all roughly hewn from the stone. The one they had followed from the cave initially had led into a much larger one that descended slowly. Logically, this was the main path down through the mountain, so they had followed it. There had been hundreds of side tunnels, which they had ignored. They probably led to the goblins' homes, their workplaces, and even their schools — if they had such things. There were markings on the tunnel walls, chiseled out of the stones, beside each of these tunnels at about shoulder height for a goblin.

"Some sort of marking system," Pixel guessed. "Cut so that they can be read by the goblins' fingers in the darkness."

"Wonderful," complained Score. "Now all we need to do is take a crash course in reading braille goblinese and we'll know what they say."

"No," Pixel said, thoughtfully. "This one's different. Look." He gestured. There were two shapes next to one another, and then the word "TRIAD."

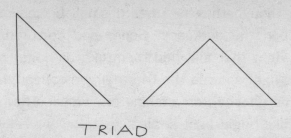

TRIAD

"Either this is English, or else it means something in the goblin language," Pixel explained. "But we've been hearing about a triad who rules the Diadem." He looked puzzled and uncomfortable. "And something inside me is telling me that this is important."

"It doesn't make any sense," Helaine objected. "Two symbols, and the word *Triad*."

"*Two* symbols," Pixel said, grinning suddenly. "But *Triad* means *three*. There's a missing symbol. So, if I fill it in . . ." He took his gemstone from his pocket. "The two symbols there are like those on your own Pages. And Oracle told us that we'd find the next Page *if you keep the crown in mind*. I'm betting that if I fill in the last symbol, then we'll get the next Page." Using the edge of his jewel, he etched a triangular shape next to the two already there.

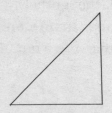

Instantly, several things happened. Huge stone blocks slammed from the ceiling behind and in front of them, blocking off any further travel. As unexpected as that was, something even stranger was happening. The wall where he'd drawn the final sign began to *melt*, rock running down like lava, to reveal a cavity in the solid rock. And inside this space sat a small box. Knowing that it was meant for him, Pixel reached in and drew the small box out. He opened it, and then grinned widely as he saw another of the Pages they were collecting within it.

The other two peered over his shoulder as he studied the sheet. As with the first two, though, it didn't seem to make any sense to him.

"Well," Pixel commented. "The piece in the top left corner is obviously the rest of the crown started on your Pages. And there's our old friend 111 again, which we've already worked out. But the rest . . ." He shook his head. "There's something odd, though." He looked at Helaine. "Let's see your Page again." When she held it next to his, Pixel grinned. "Look, on yours there's a sword and a sword with a jewel that looks brighter. On mine there's a face and a face with a jewel that looks brighter. They've got to be linked."

"We already know that the jewels increase our powers," Helaine pointed out. "It just confirms what we already knew."

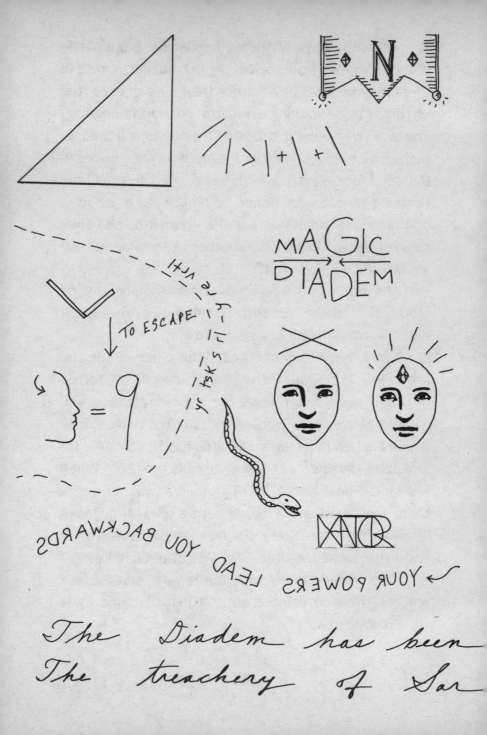

"And it also means that whoever's leaving these Pages for us doesn't know what we've learned already," Pixel replied. "These Pages must have been prepared in advance for us. Some of it's bound to overlap what we know."

"This is marvelous," complained Score. "We've got another Page, but we're trapped here now. What a trade-off."

Pixel knew what Score meant. The room they were in was fairly small. In a short while, they'd run out of fresh air. . . . He studied the rock face ahead of them, and frowned as he saw a strange thing. On a dowel jutting out from the wall were two vertical bars.

"What's this?" he asked. "Some kind of lever to open the wall again?"

"Maybe," Helaine replied. "But why spring a trap on us and leave us a way out? It doesn't make much sense." Still, she gripped the two bars and tried twisting them in all directions. Nothing seemed to make any difference, however.

There was some trick to it, obviously. Pixel studied the two bars, and then looked at his Page again. The same bars were on the Page. "TO ESCAPE," the Page read — and then pointed to a face. A face turning to equal nine. . . .

"I've got it!" Pixel exclaimed. "It's a clock face," he said. "And the time to open it is nine o'clock."

"What's a clock?" asked Helaine, puzzled.

Pixel sometimes forgot she was from a more primitive society. He gripped the hands and turned them to the right position.

With a rumble, the huge rock rose up again, freeing the path ahead of them once more.

Pixel led the way downward. They had gone along for a couple of hours, and Pixel's stomach was rumbling. He felt tired, thirsty, and cranky. More than anything else, he wanted to get out into the daylight again. This walking through the dark tunnels was getting on his nerves.

Helaine handed him a strip of her dried venison. It

was hardly appealing food, but it was better than starving. With a slight smile of thanks, he accepted the tough meat and started to chew on it. A short while later, Helaine offered both of her companions a swallow of water from the bag she carried. Once again, Pixel realized, she had been the only one who had actually been prepared for any kind of travel.

Well, it was hardly his or Score's fault. Neither of them had expected to be whisked away from their home world and thrust into this madhouse called the Diadem. Pixel tried to feel amazed that he was on his second alien planet already. But it was too depressing to get worked up about. Treen, at least, had been quite pretty when he was in its tall, stately forests. That had seemed like an alien, exotic land.

This place was just a moldy, old, extended cave. He hated it.

He stopped at the fork in the path and stared from one to the other. Both paths seemed to be equal in size, so which should they take? "Left or right?" he asked his companions.

"Beats me," Score said, as unhelpful as usual.

"Does it matter?" asked Helaine. "They both seem to have leveled off. They'll probably both take us to an exit if we follow them. As long as we get out of here, I'll be happy."

"I know what you mean," Pixel agreed, with feeling. Maybe it didn't make any difference which one they took? "Still, maybe we'd better just check the start of each one, in case there's something to tell us which is the better way to go."

Helaine shrugged. "Fine. Let's go about twenty feet down each, then come back here. I'll take the left, you two take the right." She conjured up a small light of her own and set off.

"Why should she make all the decisions?" grumbled Score. But he started down the right hand passageway anyway.

"Does it matter?" asked Pixel. "If they're good decisions, who cares?"

"I do." Score scowled. "I don't like being ordered around. I'd rather give the orders."

"I'm sure you would," Pixel agreed. "And I'm sure Helaine wouldn't like to take orders from you. Especially since she can outfight both of us."

"She seems to think that being a better fighter than us makes her a better person," Score complained. "That, and the fact that she's the daughter of some stupid Lord on her home planet. She's got too many airs and graces if you ask me."

"I didn't," Pixel answered. "And I'm sure she has just as low an opinion of you. And probably of me, as well. But you have to remember, Score, that we have to work *together*. On our own, we're not strong enough to survive on these alien planets. Together . . ." His voice trailed off as something just occurred to him. "*That's* what it means!" he exclaimed, excitedly.

"That's what *what* means?" asked Score.

"On the pages," Pixel gushed. "The bit about 111 > 1+1+1!" He was grinning almost crazily. "It doesn't mean that a hundred and eleven is greater than three! It means that three individuals together are more than simply three individuals!"

"What are you talking about?" asked Helaine, as she strode up to join them. "We were supposed to meet at the intersection, remember?"

"Never mind that," Pixel said dismissively. "It's that line on the Pages. What it means is that the sum of the three of us is greater than simply adding our individual strengths together. That if we work together, we're more than three times stronger than we are alone. We *have* to get along, and join our strengths together."

"Well, that's easier said than done," Score said sourly. "We're constantly getting on one another's nerves."

"Then we have to work on it," Pixel insisted. "We have to make an effort to work together. It won't be easy, I realize, but it's the only way that we'll ever get through this alive."

Nodding, Helaine said, "I agree. We only defeated Aranak by working as a team. We have to make every effort to stay as a team, and not splinter off again. We know just how dangerous and deadly these worlds we're on can be. If we're to survive at all, it'll be because we can work together. That means reining in your ego, Score, and not complaining all the time."

"And it means you have to stop playing little miss high and mighty," Score objected. "That really gets on my nerves."

Helaine took a deep breath, and then nodded tightly. "I'll do my best," she promised. "But just point out to me when I'm going wrong. Don't start complaining and yelling. That just makes me worse."

"There we are," said Pixel happily. "We can all get along if we try."

"Give peace a chance," muttered Score. "Okay. Then — hey! Look at that!" He gestured at the wall of the tunnel they were in.

Pixel followed his gaze, and his eyes widened when he saw what was carved into the wall there. It was the symbol for the crown again.

"This must be meant for us," he said. "It means this must be the right way."

"But why a crown?" asked Helaine, confused. "Does that refer to us somehow? Or to the Triad? Or who?"

Pixel couldn't answer that question. "Some-body's trying to help us," he said. "We must have a friend looking out for us somewhere. At least, I *hope* it's a friend."

The Shadows writhed and seethed in the air about their master. He straightened up from his view-ing mirror with a thoughtful look on his face. He rubbed his beard with his left hand and walked slowly toward the huge throne in the center of the large room. It was carved from a single, immense gem-stone, a pure diamond that sparkled and seemed al-most alive in the lights of the room.

"That boy has a point," the master mused, sitting down on the throne. "*Somebody* is helping them. They aren't intelligent enough to make sense of what the messages are saying, but that's hardly the point." He glanced up, and fixed the closest Shadow with a cold stare. "*You*," he snapped. "Do you have any idea who is sending those messages to the children?"

"No, sire," the Shadow whispered. It was caught between wanting to serve and being afraid it would be punished or destroyed for failure. "None of us have been able to detect any living person aiding them."

Its master nodded. "And nor have I," he said gently. "I can hardly fault you, then, can I? Especially since I myself can detect nothing." He slammed his fist down on the arm of the diamond throne. "No living person is helping them! And yet, somehow, they are getting clues constantly. It doesn't make any sense."

Another of the Shadows slithered forward. "Perhaps it is Shanara who is aiding them?" it suggested. "They are in her realm, after all, and we know she would love to take your place on the throne. . . ."

Its master snorted. "Shanara? That second-rate hag? She has ambition, I'll grant you, but she doesn't have the power. She relies on that lazy, fat familiar of hers to do half her work."

"Perhaps," the Shadow suggested, "it is that familiar who is aiding them? Since it isn't really human, that could be why you haven't detected anything. . . ."

The magician stared at the Shadow in amazement. "That's almost an intelligent thought," he commented. "But I had already considered it. The creature is not the one doing anything here for them. Still, you impress me with the barest glimmerings of intelligence you've shown. I want you and four others to go immediately to Rawn. Watch these humans. See if you can see who is helping them, and where these messages are coming from. But take great care not to harm the children . . . yet. Their time will come, but for now I need them alive."

"I shall not fail you, sire," the Shadow answered.

"I know you won't," its master agreed. "Because if you do I shall destroy you immediately. In great pain, I might add. Now, go." He waved his hand dismissively, and the Shadows leaped into the air, setting off on their mission.

The magician returned to his throne, lost in thought. It was strange that he found himself in the potential position of helping the three off-worlders. But he had great plans for them, and those plans would come crashing down around his ears if they died too soon. Aranak had almost ruined things by wanting their power for himself. Their victory over that fool had been surprising, but satisfying. On the other hand, Shanara was *far* more dangerous than Aranak had ever been. If it were possible, he would have gone to Rawn himself, instead of being forced to rely on the Shadows to do his bidding. They were not the brightest of servants, but they were all he had right now.

And he couldn't leave. It was ironic, but he had fought his way to where he now sat on the great throne. The position of greatest power in the whole Diadem! And he couldn't leave it. He was as trapped here as if he were a prisoner in the deepest dungeon.

At least, he was trapped until he had the children in his power. And then . . . then they would die, and he would be free once again!

CHAPTER 4

Score was getting quite impatient as they followed the latest tunnel. He was really sick of this place. For about the millionth time since he'd been thrown into this dangerous adventure, he wished he were back on the streets of New York. At least there he'd know what to do. These weird alien worlds were way outside his experience. They scared him. Still, there was definitely some compensation in this magic business. He could get quite addicted to being able to do spells and all. He fingered the emerald in his pocket and grinned. Also, if there were more jewels like this around, he could get rich. Then, when he found his way back to New York, *he'd* be the one in charge.

"Light ahead," Helaine commented, pointing. "It looks as if we found the way out after all."

"About time," Score complained. "I was starting to get claustrophobic in here. I'll even take a slice of Nature in the raw after all this stupid rock."

"Good," Pixel commented, "because that looks like what we've got."

The three of them speeded up their pace, eager to be out of the oppressive mountain. There was a low chorus of jeers behind them from the goblins. The little monsters were too scared to actually come out of their dark tunnels to fight, but they couldn't resist yelling several loud and obnoxious comments after their foes. Score didn't care — words couldn't hurt them.

And then all three of them were outside, in the sunlight again, blinking. It seemed so bright after the gloom of the caves. Score absentmindedly extinguished the floating ball of light he had created, and waited for his vision to adjust.

They were right at the foot of the mountain now, and he could see several other peaks around them. It was obviously part of a chain. Right now, though, they stood in a meadow that led down toward a forest below them. Only it was like no forest Score had ever seen.

The trees weren't green or normal colors. They

were blues, oranges, purples, and all shades in between. Aside from that, and the fact that they were huge, they seemed to be like regular trees. At least the grass was still green here, even if it was of an almost electric intensity.

"Neat," Pixel commented. "Almost like a dream."

"It's late afternoon," Helaine commented, studying the sun in the sky. Score saw that it was slightly bluish, instead of a normal yellow. This place *was* weird. "We'd better find somewhere to spend the night, preferably away from the goblins. They might come out when it's dark and come after us."

"Sounds good to me," Score agreed.

Helaine led the way down the meadow toward the trees. "I'll see if I can get us something for dinner," she said as she examined the trees. "See over there to the right? That's a trail of some sort. I doubt the goblins would have bothered making it, so it's most likely an animal trail. It'll lead you to fresh water. My water bag needs to be refilled. You and Pixel follow that path. I'll meet up with you later." They had reached the forest now, and she slipped off into the undergrowth almost soundlessly. In seconds, she had vanished.

Pixel raised an eyebrow. "You know, you have to admire her ability to do that."

Score snorted. "Getting sweet on her?" he jeered. Pixel flushed, and Score realized that maybe Pixel was. "Don't," he advised Pixel. "She's not worth it. I know we have to get along and everything, but she's a major pain in the neck."

"So are you," Pixel retorted hotly.

"Yes, I know," Score agreed easily. "Bad upbringing. What can I tell you? But I'm happy to be on my own. I do fine on my own, and as soon as we get through whatever it is we're caught up in again, I'm going to say goodbye to both of you and strike off on my own."

The two of them were following the path that Helaine had pointed out to them. Pixel said quietly, "I really don't think you're as tough and independent as you pretend. I think you're just saying that to cover up your loneliness."

"You do, huh?" Score replied. "Well, I *like* being alone. It's quieter, for one thing." He stared at Pixel pointedly. "Get the message?"

Pixel nodded. That made Score feel better. At least he wouldn't have to listen to the other kid spouting nonsense as they walked.

And it *was* nonsense. Okay, right now he needed Pixel and Helaine. But that was just temporary. Once this adventure was over, he was finished with the pair of them. He'd walk away and not look back. No regrets, no ties, nothing that could come back and cause him any harm later.

He couldn't trust other people. He had never been able to trust his father — and Bad Tony was now in jail, out of Score's life. He hadn't been able to trust his mother — when he had needed her most, she had died on him. And the people he knew from the streets — if you trusted them, they'd have stuck a knife in you and robbed you. No, he couldn't trust other people at all. Pixel and Helaine couldn't be an exception to this rule.

Could they?

In silence, they finally reached a river. It was about half a mile across, but flowing fairly peacefully. It looked wonderfully fresh, and there were the occasional glints of light in the water that had to be fish. Score wondered if it would be possible to catch some. Nice fresh fish steaks roasted on a fire would be pretty nice . . . Score really missed finding fast food restaurants on every street corner. Not that there were any streets or corners on this world.

Pixel gestured upstream slightly. "There's a clearing up there," he said. "Nice and rocky, so it should be safe to make a fire there. And we'll be away from the water spot."

"Why would we want to be?" asked Score. "If we camp here, we could catch any animals that want water, and build up some food reserves."

"Unless it was a lion or something that came," Pixel pointed out.

Score hadn't thought of that. "Maybe you're right," he agreed. "Well, I guess we'd better gather some wood for a fire. Whatever Helaine catches will need to be cooked." He didn't much like the idea of working, but there was no real option here. He could conjure up a magic fire, of course, but that wouldn't be so good for cooking over. Wood gave the food a better flavor.

By the time they had a fire started, Helaine had returned with food and a pelt. It wasn't long before the scent of the cooking steaks had Score drooling. He was already hungry from the efforts of the day, and he was almost ready to eat the steaks half-raw.

Pixel had stripped the bark off a fallen log, and washed it thoroughly in the river. "Plates," he announced. "Sorry I can't do anything about knives and forks."

"Fingers will do," Score answered.

It was almost early evening when they were done. Helaine settled down, cross-legged, and pulled the Book of Magic from her pouch. "It's nice to get the chance to have a look at this now," she commented.

"I know it's very important to us, even if I don't know how I know."

"It's like those messages we keep getting," Pixel commented. "We know things we shouldn't, and can't explain how."

"Yes," Score agreed. He held up his emerald. "I've been dreaming of this for weeks now, and I can almost feel it calling to me. But I don't know *why*."

"Maybe the book can help," Helaine said. "Let's see." She opened it up. Score and Pixel stared over her shoulders.

Score groaned. "Not again," he complained. The Page was completely unintelligible.

"Another code," Pixel said cheerfully. "You were expecting something else by now? You *know* we have to work for everything in these worlds. Let's just see what we can do."

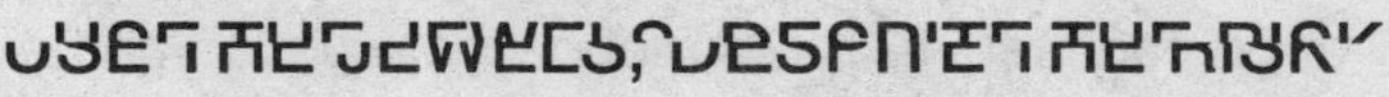

"This doesn't make any sense," Helaine said glumly.

"Wait a second," Pixel responded, staring at the code thoughtfully. "I think it's easier than we think. We just have to rearrange the shapes in our minds, and they're bound to fit into a pattern."

"What if they don't?" Score asked.

"Don't think 'don't,'" Pixel advised. "Look for a way."

Score stared hard at the code. Soon, the shapes were swimming across the page. He tried to make them match up, but it wasn't working.

Pixel had better luck.

After a few minutes, he cried, "I've got it." He quickly pulled a pen from his supply bag and proceeded to decode the message.

"It's simple," Pixel said as he wrote. "The letters have been cut in half and shifted. So if you take the top half and shift it over to match up with the bottom half, you get a message."

Within minutes, Score, Helaine, and Pixel knew what that message was.

USE THE JEWELS, DESPITE THE RISK

"So each jewel will somehow help us . . . and distort the way we communicate," Pixel summed up, after reading the full section.

"But how?" Score asked.

"Well," Helaine said, "now that we've figured out the code, let's see if the book has anything to say about gemstones." She flicked through the headings, and then stopped in triumph. "Here we are! Just the thing."

Together, they read:

"Gemstones can amplify the powers of wizards. By focusing your thoughts and energies through the jewel, your abilities will be increased greatly. The following jewels have the following properties:

1) Jasper (Green): Sight. The ability to see at great distances.

2) Sapphire (Blue): Levitation. Either of objects or oneself.

3) Agate (Brown): Communication. Telepathy with another person or creature.

4) Emerald (Green): Transmutation. Changing objects from one thing to another.

5) Onyx (Black & White): Shape-Shifting. Changing oneself or others into animals, etc, and back.

6) Ruby (Red): Finding. The ability to discover where any named object is.

7) Chrysolite (Olive Green): Water. Control over the element of Water.

8) Beryl (Blue-Green): Air. Control over the element of Air.

9) Topaz (Yellow): Fire. Control over the element of Fire.

10) Chrysoprase (Apple Green): Earth. Control over the element of Earth.

11) Jacinth (Red-Orange): Calling. The power to bring someone or something to you.

12) Amethyst (Purple): Size. The ability to change an object's size."

"All right!" exclaimed Score. "Finally, something that can help us!" He eyed his emerald eagerly. "The color of my dreams now makes sense. And this will increase the power of my ability to transform things. Instead of just small things, who knows what I'll be able to do?"

"And with my ruby," Pixel said, "I can find things. I can see that could be very helpful."

"And my sapphire can do levitation," breathed Helaine. "Well, I think we should all start to practice with what we have; now we know what they can do."

"It's just a shame we don't have more gems," Score said. "I mean, if we had more, just look at some of those wild things we could do with them."

"How are we going to get hold of any gemstones?" Pixel asked. He held up his ruby. "We're lucky to have been given these. They'd cost a fortune to buy anywhere on any of our worlds, I'm sure. And, you may notice, there are no shops here. Even if we had any money, which we don't. And even if the locals would let us have them, which isn't likely."

"Maybe not," Helaine said thoughtfully. "But I

know who might well have plenty of gems. The goblins." She glanced at her companions. "They dig all their tunnels through the earth. I'm sure they must have found and probably stockpiled plenty of gems."

"They're hardly likely to agree to *give* us any-thing — except a knife in the back," Pixel pointed out.

Score grinned. "I could always sneak back and steal some. There are advantages to having nimble fin-gers, you know." He flexed his hand. "Like you said, I'm a thief and a sneak. Sometimes that comes in handy."

"Not in the goblin tunnels," Helaine answered. "You're at too much of a disadvantage there. Besides, despite your thieving nature, I wouldn't feel right about stealing, even from goblins. Maybe we could trade with them somehow."

"How?" asked Score. "What could we give them that they might possibly want?"

"I don't know," admitted Helaine. "But it's worth thinking about, surely?"

Pixel snorted. "Well, we could always ask them," he sniggered. "But I don't think they'll give us a very civil reply. I think it would just be asking for trouble. After all, we've got three gems, and it's likely to take a while until we figure out how to use them. Why get greedy?"

"It's not greed," Score answered, irritated. "These are the first things we've found that actually give us an edge. A weapon, if you like. We should make the most of it." He looked to Helaine for support. "You're the warrior," he said. "Doesn't that make sense to you?"

"Yes," she agreed. "Surprisingly enough, I'm in complete agreement with you there. The better armed for magic we are, the better chance we have of surviving." She looked at Pixel. "You're out-voted here."

Pixel flushed, and Score couldn't help grinning. Just as Score was enjoying the situation immensely, he heard a roaring sound from further down the river. The three of them whirled around, Helaine jumping to her feet and replacing the Book of Magic in her bag.

Coming into sight around a bend in the river was a party of figures — maybe twenty of them, all in all. Score stared closely. Evening was starting to fall, but there was something very wrong about the group. Then it clicked — they were all so tall. They had to be at least seven feet, and heavily built. Several of them were howling and gesturing toward the three travelers.

"Uh-oh," Score said, uneasily. "I don't think this is the local welcome wagon."

"They sound *very* unwelcoming to me," agreed Pixel.

"And they seem to have been looking for us," Helaine added. "They're very excited to see us."

One of the figures stumbled into a small tree, only twenty or so feet tall. Enraged, the person wrapped his arms about the tree and heaved.

It came out of the ground, roots and all.

The three of them stared, astonished, as the creature whirled the tree angrily about its head and then threw it into the river with a great splash.

Score swallowed nervously. "Guys," he said, his voice shaking, "I don't think we're going to stand a chance here."

Even Helaine looked pale. "Just this once, I'm voting in favor of Score's favorite strategy. Time to run away."

That relieved Score. He turned to start running, and then groaned. "Cancel that thought," he said, shaking.

A second group of the creatures was heading at them from the other direction. They were all drawing closer, and Score could make out their ugly features, and their bad breath.

"Giant trolls," Helaine muttered. "I've heard stories about them. Dumb, but incredibly strong and virtually unstoppable."

"That I needed to hear?" Score asked. "Now what?"

The trolls gave a concerted roar of anger and then all of them started to rush toward the trio, ready to tear them into very small pieces and to stomp those pieces into the ground.

CHAPTER 5

Helaine couldn't help feeling a pang of fear as she saw the giant trolls charge. She had her sword in her hand almost by reflex, even though she knew it wouldn't do her much good. According to legends, it was extremely difficult to stop a single troll — let alone almost thirty of them. If she had fifty of her father's armored fighting men with her, they might have stood some chance. But with just Score and Pixel?

They were doomed.

Still, she was the daughter of a Lord, and a warrior. She refused to scream, panic, or hide in terror. She would face her death with dignity, and her sword in hand.

"You're thinking this all wrong!" Pixel insisted. "We've got to get used to the fact that we're *magic-users* now. We can't take on these trolls in hand-to-hand combat. Put that stupid sword down, and let's use our best weapon: magic."

Helaine was amazed. Pixel was absolutely correct: that was their only chance. She still couldn't get used to thinking of herself as a magic-user, though. But she had to. She sheathed her sword and pulled out her sapphire instead. She'd hoped for time to get used to this, but there wasn't any left to her. If she didn't get it right now, there would be no more chances.

The sapphire was supposed to amplify her powers of levitation, so . . . she focused her thoughts on the bunch of trolls closest to them. There were six of them, howling and rushing up the hill with surprising speed for creatures so big and bulky. Their mass was clearly all muscle and not fat. Concentrating hard, she raised the gem to eye level and pushed outward with her mind.

Rise . . . rise . . .

For a second, it looked as if nothing was happening. Then she saw that the trolls were losing their balance, and flailing around with their arms. Their huge, hairy feet were several inches off the ground, and tipping the trolls over backward. It was almost comical to see them floundering several inches off the ground, screaming curses and threats. But they could do nothing to continue their attack like that. There was no way they could get down, and nothing for them to grab hold of to stop themselves from rising higher.

Pixel's gem wasn't much help here. Ruby was for finding things, and that wouldn't stop a troll. Instead, taking a leaf from Score's book, Pixel was creating and launching burning balls of fire at the closest trolls. Beside him, Score had his emerald out, and was focusing his thoughts through it. Out of the corner of her eye, Helaine saw a pit open in the ground in front of three trolls, and they plunged into it. Score must have transformed the earth into gas! They *did* stand a chance, after all.

But there were still more than twenty trolls drawing closer. Helaine switched her attention to the next closest clump of attackers. As she did so, the first six she'd levitated crashed back to earth. They were stunned for a moment because of the sudden drop, but then they staggered back to their feet.

Helaine fumed. The levitation only worked while she was concentrating directly on the trolls. As soon as she switched elsewhere, the effects wore off. Well, they had a few seconds before the first trolls managed to get back into action. She concentrated again on the next bunch, and picked five of them up into the air. Then she pushed them with her mind. They went flying out over the river, and she switched off the power.

With loud splashes and yells, they all fell into the water. Judging from their general air of filth and untidiness, this was not a popular pastime with the trolls. That should keep them out of the battle for a while, at least!

But the rest were almost on them now, despite the best efforts of Helaine, Pixel, and Score. They were going to be overwhelmed, and then torn apart!

"Not *them*," Pixel gasped, his face straining from the magic he was using. "Lift *us*!"

Of course! Why hadn't this occurred to her? She still wasn't thinking magically at all. She focused her attention now on the three of them, and they shot up twenty feet into the air, and hung there, above the furious trolls. For a second, they were safe.

Then one troll hauled a boulder out of the ground and threw it up at them. Score quickly changed it to water, which splashed down on the angry trolls. But with this idea in mind, the trolls split up and started grabbing rocks, small trees, and anything else at hand and began to bombard the three of them with their makeshift missiles.

"We can't keep ducking this stuff," gasped Score, changing a small sapling into a shower of roses. The magic use was draining them all now. Helaine could feel the strain of keeping them aloft. She knew she wouldn't be able to keep it up for very much longer.

"Myb cn fly s vr th rvr," she suggested. "Th trlls dn't lk wtr mch."

"What are you saying?" Score asked desperately.

"Wht? 'm gng t try t fly s vr th rvr."

"She's not making any sense," Score looked to Pixel.

"Wait. I think using the sapphire is affecting her speech. Like in the Book of Magic — she's lost her vowels.

"Rlly?" Helaine asked. Obviously, she couldn't sense the difference.

"Yes," Pixel nodded. "Repeat what you said."

"Lt's fl vr th rvr."

"Fly over the river?"

"Ys."

"Worth a try," Score agreed.

She focused her thoughts again to moving them. But it was slow work, and it wasn't very smooth. She knew with practice she'd get better at this, but right now it was all she could do to keep them up and moving slowly.

"We need some sort of distraction," Pixel said. "I'm going to look at that Book of Magic." He fished it out of her bag, almost upsetting her concentration as he did so. As she moved them toward the river, he flicked through the Pages.

"Here's one!" he announced happily. "Illusion casting! If we make them think they're being attacked by something else, that should occupy them while we escape."

"Y nd Scr d t," Helaine gasped, sweat trickling down her forehead. "t's hrd t kp s p hr."

"Hard to keep us up here." Pixel showed Score the Page, and together they began to concentrate on the spell. This meant that neither of them was blocking the troll's missiles now, and several rocks came perilously close to them.

Then even Helaine felt the outpouring of magic from the spell. For a second, it felt as if her heart had stopped, and then the three of them plummeted back to the ground. Helaine had just enough strength left to break their falls before they broke bones hitting the earth.

The magic had gone wrong again, just as it had that time on Treen. She had *felt* the wrongness of the spell. Helaine knew it had happened this time, and it had drained strength from her as well. She didn't have the power to levitate anything right now, which spelled big trouble.

The misfired magic spelled even worse trouble.

Score and Pixel had been trying to create the illusion of a small dragon and a large manticore attacking the trolls.

Instead, they had somehow conjured up a whole bevy of small, nasty monsters — all of them terribly real. Some of them had multiple mouths and appetites to match. Others had claws and tentacles that reached out for whatever was closest. There had to be hundreds of the small, misshapen, nasty creatures. A lot of them attacked the trolls, which helped the trio. But the rest turned their attention to the humans.

Slobbering, teeth-grinding *things* scuttled across the ground toward the three of them. Helaine whipped out her sword, and hacked the closest one in two as she scrambled to her feet. Score and Pixel were throwing firebombs at others. But it was clearly hopeless. There were just too many of the horrible monsters.

Helaine slashed out again, spearing and chopping at anything she could reach. Despite this, one of the things got close enough to bite her ankle, even through her boot. She felt a second of searing pain before she managed to gut the creature with her sword. It fell away, dead, but the scent of her fresh blood in the air seemed to inflame its fellow creatures to even greater frenzy.

Blood trickled into her boot from her wound,

which felt as if it were on fire. But Helaine concentrated her energies, refusing to acknowledge the pain. She managed to block a lot of it from her consciousness, but she knew it couldn't last. She'd pay for it later — if she were still alive later.

The trolls were stomping on monsters as fast as they could, but more and more were pouring out of somewhere and falling on them. Yelling in pain and anger, the trolls tried to retreat. Then Helaine's attention was fully taken with fighting off the monsters close at hand. She felt sorry for the trolls, but there was nothing she could do for them.

There wasn't much she could do for herself, either.

Pixel screamed as one of the monsters bit his arm. Helaine managed to spear the thing with her sword and throw it free, but Pixel was hurt quite badly from the bite. Blood was trickling down his arm, and his face was screwed up with pain. Still, he fought on, blasting fire as fast as he could make it. Helaine noticed almost in passing that Score had a gash in his leg, too. They were all going to be cut down by these monsters, killed in slow stages, one bite after another . . . and there was nothing they could do to stop it.

They were doomed.

However, she wasn't going down without a fight,

and she kept battling on. Her sword was getting wet with monster blood and her own sweat, and now and then she felt another painful nip from a fast biter that she managed to kill. But it seemed to be simply routine now. Hack, slice, fight, and keep going.

Then, abruptly, there was a lull in the fighting. There were still plenty of monsters left, but they were hanging back from the trio. Helaine gasped, her breath burning her lungs, she was so exhausted. "What's with them?"

"Maybe," panted Pixel, "they're scared of us."

"Or something else," Score said. But what?

And then Helaine saw what. Screaming down from the darkening sky were what looked like solidified shadows. It was hard to make out any real shape — but she had the impression of lots of claws and teeth, as well as wings and eyes. But only while she wasn't directly looking at them. If she looked straight at them, it was like a patch of *nothing* hanging in the air.

"The Shadows!" Pixel breathed. "It has to be the Shadows. Remember, the Beastials said that whoever was behind the whole plot against us controlled these creatures he called Shadows?"

"Oh, great," Score complained, his face pale. "Just what we need — more trouble. I guess we're lucky we can only die once."

Helaine raised her sword again. She had no idea whether or not the Shadows could even be touched by her blade, but she was going to try. If they could cut her with their claws — if they had claws — then she could get them with her weapon. Then she frowned slightly, as she realized that the Shadows weren't aiming for them.

Down from the sky, the Shadows plunged into the monsters that were now starting to panic. Black traces of the Shadows' bodies seemed to tear through the creatures as though they were paper, throwing grisly bits of corpses in all directions.

"They're *helping* us," Pixel breathed, stunned. "But why?"

"Who cares?" Score asked. "Look, guys, the monsters have kept the trolls occupied, and the Shadows are keeping the monsters off us. I say we take the opportunity to run for our lives."

"Seconded," Helaine agreed hastily. "Though I'm not sure how long I'll be able to actually run."

"I know what you mean," Pixel replied. "Let's go as long as we can."

They turned and ran, Helaine taking the lead. They couldn't cross the river, since it was too wide at this point and it was getting too dark to see their way across. And the trolls had come from downstream, which tended to suggest that was where their homes were — and possibly reinforcements, too. That left only one direction for them to flee in — back the way they had come.

"You're leading us back to the goblins," Score complained, gasping as he struggled to keep up.

"What choice do we have?" Helaine demanded. "We'll have to hope they're still too scared of us to attack us, and maybe we can go the other way past their caves when it gets light."

"She's right," Pixel agreed. "At the moment, it's the least dangerous alternative."

"Maybe," Score grumbled, "but I for one would appreciate a zero danger alternative." But then he shut up and concentrated on making the best speed he could.

Helaine was almost totally drained, and her ankle hurt quite badly. The other scratches and scrapes she'd suffered weren't helping either. She knew that almost all of her magical strength was gone, too. She had barely enough left to conjure up a glowing ball of light and send it in front of them. They badly needed to be able to see where they were going. The last thing they needed now was for one of them to trip and break an ankle, or simply run into a tree or boulder.

She had no idea how long they continued on. Sweat was pouring down her face and back now, and her ankle felt as if it had been broken. At least it had stopped bleeding, though. There was drying blood in her boot, which made it difficult and painful to move — but it would be worse if she stopped. The night was getting very dark now, and a sprinkling of stars in unfamiliar constellations broke out whenever the branches overhead cleared enough for her to see the sky.

And there were two small moons rising, both bright and almost cheerful, but smaller than the ones she was used to back home. It simply reinforced how alien this planet really was, for all of its similarities to home.

Finally, the stitch in her side was burning her up, and she could go no further. "I've got to stop," she gasped, and virtually collapsed onto the ground.

"Thank you," Pixel replied, heavy and straining as he fell down beside her. "I didn't want to be the first to stop, but I'm wiped."

"Me too," agreed Score, dropping beside them. He, too, looked to be in great pain, and sweat had made his clothes stick to his skinny body. "Are we far enough away, do you think?"

"We have to be," Helaine informed him, "because I seriously doubt we're any of us is up to traveling any further tonight. We've got to have rest, and we have to try to see to our wounds." She sat up, breathing slightly easier, and tried to favor her injured foot. "How badly off are the two of you?"

Score winced. Helaine expected a list of whining complaints from him, but instead he just shrugged. "Not too bad," he confessed. "A few bites here and there, that's all. You two look worse."

"I'll survive," Pixel said. He examined his cuts and scratches, and then scowled. "It might be an idea to wash the wounds, though, so they don't get infected. The teeth on those things we accidentally created didn't look too hygienic." He glanced at Helaine. "You don't happen to have any magic helpers in that bag of yours, do you?"

"That bag of mine," she replied, "is back at our campsite. So is the water skin, and all the food." She couldn't keep the bitterness out of her voice. "All we've got left is whatever we've got on us. We've lost everything else."

CHAPTER 6

Pixel could hear the disgust and despair in Helaine's voice. She seemed to take it as a personal failure that she'd been forced to leave their supplies behind. It was silly of her, because there had been absolutely no time to try and gather anything up. She was expecting too much from herself.

"Then we'll just have to do without," he answered. "I'm sure you'll be able to go hunting in the morning and get us some more food, and a new water skin. You've still got your bow and arrows, after all."

"Yes," she agreed, not molified at all. "But I don't think I'm going to be doing much hunting for a few days." She winced with pain as she pulled her boot down off her left ankle.

Pixel gasped with shock as he saw that the whole joint was a mass of congealing blood. "Why didn't you say you'd been hurt so badly?" he demanded, concerned.

"There wasn't time while we were running for our lives," Helaine responded drily. "But I don't think I'm going much further for a while."

"You are not," Pixel scolded her. He bent to look at her wound. He could see that the ankle was swelling badly. That was a result of her putting so much strain on it. "We've got to get this seen to," he said firmly. "Otherwise it's going to give you trouble."

Helaine managed a weak grin. "Too late," she muttered.

"We need water," Pixel said. He looked around. "But we're not going to find any in this darkness." He felt so helpless.

Score gave one of his sarcastic sighs. "I thought you claimed to be the brains of this bunch," he scoffed, and then grinned at Pixel. "What's the magical power of that jewel you're carrying?"

Pixel felt like banging his head against a rock. *Of course!* How could he have forgotten? "Finding . . ."

he murmured. "You're right, I should have thought of that."

"Good thing one of us is on the ball," Score replied smugly, obviously proud of himself. "So, go find water."

Pixel pulled out his ruby and held it in his hands. He stared into its depths, seeing the flash of lights that Helaine's ball of fire was still giving out. "Retaw," he said to the jewel. "Ew deen retaw."

Just as the Book had said — the ruby made him speak backwards!

Instantly, a bright beam of light shone like a laser from one side of the crystal. It shot into the darkness, a guideline to the nearest water. "Ti skrow!" he exclaimed. "Lla ew evah ot od si ot wollof eht maeb."

Helaine groaned. "The jewel is pointing back the way we just came," she said. "The river must be the closest water. That doesn't help us at all."

Feeling deflated by this observation, Pixel tried to concentrate on what the ruby was finding. An image of the river and their abandoned campsite came to his mind, as clearly as if he were looking at it in front of him. "Er'uoy thgir," he agreed miserably. "I nac ees eht ecalp won." It was just like Virtual Reality, almost as if he could reach out and grasp their abandoned supplies. The trolls, the monsters and the Shadows all seemed to have vanished now. He didn't want to examine what the squelchy-looking leftovers were. But this didn't help him because he couldn't get anything. His magic just told him where it was. It couldn't bring anything to them.

Unless . . .

"We have to start thinking properly," Pixel said after putting the jewel down. "Like we said earlier, we're still not realizing that we're magic-users. We're thinking too conventionally."

"Well," Score said, "that sounds good, but what do you *mean*?"

"I mean that we can't *physically* go back to the river for water," Pixel explained. "But we shouldn't have to. If we can do magic, then we can get the water other ways."

"At the moment," Helaine interrupted, "I can barely stay awake, let alone do magic."

"You've done enough," Pixel assured her. "Rest for a bit. But will you allow me to use your sapphire for awhile? I'm the least exhausted of us, and there's something I want to try."

Helaine looked for a second as if she might refuse. Pixel could understand why. Already he felt as if his ruby were somehow a part of him, and that giving it to someone else would be like loaning them his hand. But then she nodded, and passed it to him. She didn't have to say *look after it, or else*, because it was in the look she gave him. He smiled reassuringly at her.

"Now, just try to rest a bit," he told her. "I'll see what I can do." He glanced up at Score. "Maybe you could keep an eye out for trouble?" he suggested. "It looks like we're safe for now, but I'm not willing to gamble my life on that."

"Me neither," agreed Score. He clambered slowly to his feet. "Okay, I'll take first watch, while you do . . . whatever you're trying." Almost pleasantly, he nodded, and then moved away.

Holding his ruby in his right hand and Helaine's sapphire in his left, Pixel opened up his thoughts again. Immediately, he could see their former camp-site, and the abandoned provisions. Water was the biggest need. Thankfully, Helaine had refilled her water skin shortly before the attack. It lay beside the almost-dead campfire. Scattered around were several haunches of venison, and then Pixel could see Helaine's supply bag.

Would this work? Pixel honestly had no idea, but they badly needed those supplies, and he couldn't think of any other way to get them. "Seeing" them in his mind's eye, he then focused his thoughts through the sapphire.

Rise . . . rise . . .

He wasn't as good at this as Helaine was. The

sapphire was somehow hers, after all, but he had the same power she did. And the jewel amplified it. Tied in with the finding magic of the ruby, Pixel could feel his mind reach out to encompass the water skin, the provision bag, and the deer hide and meat. Could he really do it, or was he just fooling himself?

Nothing happened. Frustrated, Pixel growled in the back of his throat. "The sapphire won't work for me," he complained.

"Then I guess I'll have to do that part after all," Helaine said firmly, reclaiming her stone. "We'll just have to link together to do it." There was so much steel in her voice that Pixel didn't dare argue. He sat beside her, concentrating on seeing the scene, and sharing it with Helaine. She nodded, and then focused on her own jewel.

Slowly, the items started to twitch where they lay in the grass. Then, slowly, they began to rise into the air. It was very shaky, but it was happening.

It took a while, and Pixel could feel Helaine shaking with the strain. Eventually, though, Score gave a cry as he saw the supplies slide into view. As he did so, Helaine gasped. "Cn't d ny mr," she murmured, and collapsed into sleep. The supplies nose-dived into the grass, and Score went to collect them.

Score brought them back, and then concentrated. A ball of fire sprang to life several feet away.

He placed some meat near it to heat through. "I don't know about you," he explained, "but all that fighting and running made me hungry again. I'm going to want a midnight snack . . ."

He then crossed to where Helaine had fallen into a deep sleep. Score snorted to himself, and poured some of the water over her ankle. Pixel had been certain that it would wake her, but she was obviously too far drained. She slept on. Pixel was too exhausted himself to help out, and his stomach was grumbling. Score had been right — they had been totally drained by the fight and flight. Food was a good idea.

Score tore a strip off his T-shirt and used it to clean Helaine's ankle. Pixel could see that the teeth marks were inflamed, and the ankle itself swollen. One thing was certain — Helaine wasn't going to be doing much traveling on that foot for a while. He doubted that she'd even be able to get her boot back on in the morning. Score then poured some water all over his washcloth, and concentrated on it. Pixel grinned as he saw the cloth freeze. Smart move! Score wrapped the icy bandage around Helaine's ankle. That would help the swelling at least a little.

Then Score brought some of the slightly burned meat to share. They ate hungrily for a short while, taking the edge off their starvation. Then Pixel asked, "What do you think of her ankle?"

Score shrugged. "It's cute, but I've seen nicer."

"That's not what I meant!"

Grinning, Score punched him lightly on the shoulder. "I knew that. Just kidding." Then he sobered up. "I'd say she'll be lucky if she can walk on it soon. Then again, I'm no doctor, so maybe I'm wrong. Let's face it, if Helaine decides to do something, there's not a lot in this world, or any other, that she lets stop her, is there?"

"No," Pixel agreed. He couldn't help admiring Helaine more than any other girl he had ever known. He didn't think he was really getting a crush on her, as Score seemed to think. But he couldn't help liking and respecting her. "So, you're getting to respect her, too?"

Score snorted. "Not hardly. But she's not such a pain as I first thought, I guess. She did okay running around with her ankle in that shape, and she never let on once how it must have been hurting her." Then he shook himself. "But enough about her favorite subject. You showed that these gems are pretty specifically bound to only one of us. We need to get some more."

"The first thing we need," Pixel answered, "is some kind of a plan. I mean, all we've done so far is to either run into trouble or away from it. Whatever's going on, other people are controlling our lives. I for one don't much care for that. I want to be the one in charge here. We have to make plans first thing in the morning, after we're rested, and decide just what our goals are. Then we have to figure how to get to them."

"Sounds good to me," agreed Score. "But right now, I think my brain's on an extended vacation. You look wiped. Get some rest. I'll wake you up in a few hours, so I can sleep. I think one of us had better stay on watch, just in case." He cast Helaine an almost sympathetic look. "And I don't think it should be her."

"Agreed," said Pixel, relieved. He was so tired, he really had to get some rest. Everything had taken just too much out of him, he had to . . . sleep.

Unseen by the humans, there were watchers in the trees.

"Humans," one of them said in disgust. He shifted his footing slightly, and raised his spear. "We should kill them now, and have done with it."

"No," his leader answered, flicking a long, elegant tail without conscious thought. "I must confess that they intrigue me."

"Intrigue you?" The first speaker snorted, and stomped a hoof — not loud enough for the humans to hear him, though. "They disgust me. You *know* that humans are always trouble. We centaurs have wisely elected to have nothing at all to do with them."

"Killing them would be having something to do with them," his leader replied mildly. He nodded at the clearing ahead. "They've battled trolls and goblins, and they're still alive. That's quite an achievement, Rothar. Could *you* do it? Honestly?"

Rothar twitched, uncomfortably. "Perhaps not," he conceded. "But I still think they'll cause trouble, Dethrin."

"So do I," agreed Dethrin. "But I'd sooner avoid it if possible. If they can defeat trolls and goblins, maybe they can defeat centaurs, too."

"Wisely spoken, my brother."

The two male centaurs turned slightly to greet Dethrin's sister as she approached. Like Dethrin, her lower body was a deep black, trim horse's shape. But a human body, arms, and head rose from this. These were also black, as was her long, manelike hair that grew from her head and down her spine. Dethrin had always thought his sister to be a rare beauty, and he knew from the response of Rothar beside him that this was a view shared by many of the males.

"Amaris," murmured Rothar. He was a white centaur, and colored almost unnoticeably in the darkness. "It is good to see you again. I was not aware that you were joining us."

Laughing, she shook her mane. "You know me — restless as ever. I just had to see what was going on."

She peered through the gap in the branches. "Three humans? And children, by the look of them. They seem harmless enough."

"Don't let their docile appearances fool you," Rothar warned. "They're more dangerous than they look. They have to be, to have survived this long. They've already battled trolls and goblins, and won."

"Really?" Amaris flicked her tail almost flirtatiously. "And how many of the foe have they slaughtered?"

Dethrin broke in. "That's what interests me. As far as I can tell, they haven't killed a single one. Oh, they've given them a good beating, but they've not actually killed anyone."

"They hacked up a lot of monsters," Rothar pointed out.

"Ones that they accidentally created," argued Dethrin. "Even in hiding, I could feel their magic go wrong."

Amaris sighed. "That's still happening?" she asked.

"Yes," her brother replied. "And these three are novices at best. But they don't seem to be as . . . predatory as most humans. So I've given the order just to watch them, and not to harm them. Yet. Unless they prove to be directly dangerous to us."

"They will," Rothar said darkly. "Mark my words, they will."

"If that is the case," Dethrin said firmly, "then we shall kill them. Until then, we only watch. Is that clear?" Rothar didn't immediately reply. "Is that clear?" Dethrin repeated, this time with an edge to his voice.

"Yes," Rothar finally agreed, obviously with regret. "Though only for the time being. They'll be trouble. You mark my words — humans always are."

CHAPTER 7

Score was dreaming, but he knew that it was more than a dream. It was a vision of some kind, and he knew it was important. He could see his mother, the way she had looked when he was a child, and she was walking toward him. As she drew closer, though, she started to split apart, and became three people walking toward him. Her face and body changed, and Score saw that it was now two men and a woman he didn't know who were drawing closer. They were all dressed in long, flowing robes that were very rich and patterned. Their faces were middle-aged, and their expressions terribly cold.

And then they shimmered and vanished. In their

place was a sheet of paper, fluttering in the air. Score knew instantly that it was another of the Pages. He reached toward it, wishing he could see what was on it. It was snatched away from him by a cloaked, shadowy person. He tried to call out for him or her to give it back, but the hand clutching the paper suddenly became a bird's claw. Puzzled, he watched as it morphed into a lion's paw, and then into long, thin talons.

Score awoke feeling very sore and stiff, and under-rested. His dream was still vivid in his mind, but he saw that it was now morning. He and Pixel had alternated watches in the night, letting Helaine sleep. This meant that neither of them had really managed to get enough sleep, but there was no help for that. He'd sooner be a bit tired than have his throat cut in the night.

Pixel was still on watch, but he'd started a small, real fire. Wincing at each ache and pain he felt, Score ambled over to join his companion. He glanced at where Helaine still lay sleeping. Thankfully, it had been a mild night, so they hadn't needed any blankets.

"So, what's on the agenda for today?" Score asked, taking a drink from the water skin.

"We have to make a plan," Pixel replied. "We can't just go on letting things happen to us. This world so far seems pretty rough, but I have to admit that some of it seems to be very nice." He gestured at the oddly colored trees. "I could get used to this. If there was somewhere civilized around here to live, I wouldn't mind staying for a while."

"I don't think that's an option," Helaine broke in flatly. "Don't forget, we're definitely being hunted by somebody." Score glanced across to where she was sitting up and stretching. "So we know we have at least one foe on this world," Helaine continued. She tried to stand, and winced in pain as she stood. Her ankle was obviously swollen and hurting her badly.

"Sit down!" Score snapped, irritated. "You're just making your ankle worse, and you're not impressing us with how brave and impervious to pain you are."

Glaring at him, Helaine took a step, and then groaned with pain and fell to the ground. "I'd strike for that, but you'd have to come over here," she complained. Pixel jumped to his feet and hurried to help her. "Back off," she snapped. "I don't need any help."

"Really?" Score asked drily. "What are you going to do — shuffle around on this planet on your backside? There's no shame in admitting that sometimes you *do* need a little help."

For a moment, it looked as if Helaine was going to punch him for that. Then, abruptly, she managed a grin, and nodded. "You're right," she admitted. "I could do with a hand. I'm sorry."

"That's better," Pixel said approvingly. He helped her to rise to her feet again, and supported her left side while she staggered painfully the few steps to fall down beside Score.

When their hunger had been seen to, they settled down to a council of war. "We need a plan," Pixel commented.

"You keep saying that," objected Score. "So what are we going to do? At the moment, staying alive looks to me like priority number one."

"Well, you're right there," agreed Helaine. She gestured at her ankle. "And I'm not going to be much good in a fight with my ankle like this. I can't even stand up properly."

"Which also rules out much traveling," Pixel commented. "At least, until you get a little better. So I suggest we take some time to study. With the food we've got left, all we need is a supply of water and we should be okay here for a couple of days. I didn't see anything while I was on watch last night, so we might possibly be safe to stay here."

Helaine glanced around. "It's a bit too exposed for my liking," she observed. "Maybe the goblins didn't attack last night, but that doesn't mean they might not rediscover their courage and come at us again. If we're camping out, I'd rather be where we can defend ourselves in case of trouble."

"It'll be slow going if we have to move you," Pixel complained.

"Let her move herself," Score grumbled. "Her ankle's only swollen, not gone."

"Trust you to be so unsympathetic," Pixel retorted.

"Well, at least I'm not mooning over her!" Score snapped back. That made Pixel blush brightly, but it seemed to go right over Helaine's head. "Anyway, I'm not being unsympathetic — just practical. She says we can't stay here, so we have to find a way to get her moving, that's all."

"Maybe by magic?" Helaine suggested. "I've got the sapphire, after all, and that enables me to levitate. I could simply float along and keep up with you."

"See?" Score said to Pixel. "All we have to do is think."

"Arguing isn't going to get us anywhere," Helaine broke in. "So, what about setting some kind of plan? We need a goal to work toward."

Pixel seemed to have finally managed to get his embarrassment under control. "Well, we've been at the mercy of whoever is attacking us so far," he explained. "Everything that happened to us on Treen was because of this. And our being here on Rawn is obviously part of his, her, their, or its plan. So we should try and derail that."

"And how do we do that?" asked Score.

"Through a Portal," Pixel said. "That's how the trips between worlds are made. So we have to find out how to make our own Portal. If we can get off Rawn, then we'll at least be on neutral ground. This place has to be part of our unknown enemy's plans for us, so we're bound to be better off if we leave it."

"That makes sense," agreed Helaine. "It's always bad tactics to allow your foes to select the battlefield. But where do we go to?"

"Does it matter?" asked Score. "For one thing, anywhere else has to be *our* choice. And, for another, this is all hypothetical. We don't have the vaguest idea how to create a Portal. And I got the impression from the Beastials that it's something only a skilled magician can do. And, let's face it, we might be magic-users, but we're far from skilled."

"Why are you always so negative?" snapped Pixel.

"No," Helaine said, unexpectedly. "He's right, for once. This business of a Portal is likely to be very hard. But maybe we can approach it in stages. First of all, we need to know *how* it's done." She tapped the Book of Magic. "Maybe this will tell us how. I think we'd better at least skim through it and see what subjects it covers. The two of you will have to find somewhere for us to move to. It needs to be near drinking water, and to have either a cave, or a hill, or something where we can't be snuck up on. If we have to face foes, we have to have them come at us in one direction only."

Score didn't like the idea of working with Pixel much, but Helaine was probably right. It would most likely take the two of them together to search out a good campsite. "But the closest water's the river," he objected. "And the trolls might still be there, waiting for us."

"Then look for the *second* closest," Helaine said, allowing her exasperation to show through. "Can't you think for yourselves?"

Pixel blushed again. "I didn't think of that," he apologized. "But that's a good idea." He removed the ruby from his pocket, and stared into it. After a moment, a bright beam of red light shone out of it toward what Score decided to call the North. Thankfully, it didn't point either to the mountains or the river. "S'ti tuoba . . . xis selim ffo," Pixel said, as he attuned to the source. "S'ti emos dnik fo a ekal, I kniht."

"That sounds perfect," Helaine agreed. "Well, we'd better get packed. I'll come along with you till we reach the lake. Then you'll have to scout out a campsite for us while I check the Book." She took her sapphire from her pouch and concentrated. Her boot flew across to her. She tried to pull it on, but Score could see it wouldn't work. Her ankle was still too swollen. Instead, she tucked it through her belt.

Score helped to pack the rest of their meat into the dried deer skin, and used a length of leather that Helaine handed him to make it into a kind of sack, which he slung over his shoulders. Helaine then pulled on her bow and quiver, and buckled her sword back on. Then, holding the sapphire, she managed to raise herself two feet off the ground, still in a seated position.

"Ky," she said. "Lt's hp ths jwl cn kp m p. Ths mgc s drnng n ts wn wy."

Score started off in the direction that the gem had indicated. Helaine floated after him, and Pixel brought up the rear. It was odd seeing Helaine bobbing along in the air, and having her speak in the sapphire-distorted way, but Score figured he'd better get used to it. They were now real magic-users, after all, and he couldn't let it freak him out anymore.

They managed to keep up a pretty good pace because it was quite easy in this forest. The trees still looked very wrong to him, with their bizarre colors, but it was actually quite a nice place when he stopped feeling scared of what might leap out at them. It was very different from New York, of course. The only noises here were of birds and animals in the woods or trees.

It was also oddly relaxing. Sure, his legs were aching a bit, but there was something very calming about being out in the woods like this. He might even be able to get used to it, if he had to. Despite the fact that Helaine was moving slightly slower by levitation than she would have done walking normally, they kept up a good pace. The six-mile walk, conducted mostly in silence, was over in two hours, as they arrived by the shores of a lake.

It was quite impressive, at least a mile across and a couple of miles long. There were two small islands off-shore that made Helaine's eyes sparkle.

"Thr's gd plc t st p cmp," she suggested. "Nbdy wld b bl t gt t s t sly thr. nd w cld lvtt crss t thm." Then she frowned. "n th thr hnd, thy'r vry smll, nd w'd hv t cm t shr fr fd, nd fr wd." She glanced around the shoreline. "Myb thr's smwhr bttr cls by."

"Somewhere better close by? We'll check," said Pixel cheerily. "You stay here and read the spell book. Score and I won't be too long."

"More walking," complained Score, but not too nastily. He was still feeling up to the effort. He and Pixel set off along the shore to the right, while Helaine made herself comfortable on the small beach with their supplies scattered around her.

Score wasn't entirely certain what they were looking for, and he hoped that Pixel had a better idea.

88

What did a good campsite look like? He tried to decide. "Maybe we can find a stream or river leading into the lake," he suggested. "Flowing water might be better than lake water to drink."

"A good idea," agreed Pixel. He surveyed the shoreline. "It looks like there's a stream up ahead. Let's try that." They moved on, a little more excited with the prospect ahead.

Then Score stopped, and gestured down to the sand. "Look." There was a small pile of bones beside the lake, water lapping gently over them.

Kneeling, Pixel picked up one of the larger bones. "Well, something died here," he said. "So?"

"I'm no expert," Score answered, taking the bone from the other boy. He pointed to several deep grooves on it. "But they look like teeth marks to me, and from something pretty large. Maybe there's something dangerous around here?"

Pixel paled slightly. "Uh . . . you could be right," he agreed. "Like a lion, or something?" He glanced nervously at the trees.

"Nothing that normal," Score answered, a bad feeling creeping over him. "Lions would drag their prey off into the trees to eat it. These bones are by the water."

"Crocodiles?"

"You're thinking too normally," Score answered,

now definitely worried. "This is a world where trolls and goblins live, remember? I don't think this is just some simple little crocodile."

Pixel was as worried as Score now. He scanned the way ahead. "Looks like more bones over there," he said slowly.

"I think it's time to return to Helaine," Score decided. "She's a bit too close to the water's edge for my liking, and she's hardly in any shape to fight something that can chew animals up like this."

Pixel nodded. They turned and started to jog back to where they had left Helaine. She was barely more than a small dot at this distance, so there wasn't any point in even trying to yell a warning. Besides, Score realized, they might just be overreacting. Helaine would probably just laugh at their fears and assure them that there was nothing to be worried about.

"Look!" Pixel exclaimed, pointing out toward one of the islands. For a moment, Score couldn't see anything that he might be referring to. Then he saw in the water, close to the island, some kind of wake. There was something in the water, moving toward the beach where Helaine sat, obliviously reading her book.

They sped up now, rushing as fast at they could. But there was no way they'd beat whatever-it-was back to Helaine.

"Warn her," gasped Score. "We've got to warn her!"

"She won't hear us," Pixel answered. "Too far away."

He was right. But Score wasn't giving up. After all, they had magic powers, now. As he ran, he concentrated on forming a special fireball. "Shriker Kula prior," he muttered, between gasps for breath. When he held the fire in his hand, he then threw it, and used his magic to send it skimming across the lake toward whatever was heading for Helaine.

As it came over the fast-moving object, Score triggered the ball with his mental command. It exploded like fireworks over the thing in the water.

He saw Helaine jerk upright at this and look out across the water. Terrific! She'd seen the thing approaching her now. Then, to his dismay, he saw her pull out her sword and raise it. She was going to try to fight the creature!

Score ran as hard as he could. He couldn't let Helaine face a lake monster alone! He didn't even try to think about why he felt like that. He just had to help somehow.

And then the creature struck. Score realized that Helaine wouldn't have had time to move, which was why she was trying to fight instead. From the water, a long neck arched into the air. It was at least eighteen feet long, and the head at the end was large, with two great, staring eyes and a mouth filled with way too many teeth.

Helaine struck out at the head, which drew back, hissing so loudly that Score could hear it even at this distance. The monster reared back, humping part of its body onto the land. It was a greenish-gray color all over, with spines running down the neck and across its back. A huge tail churned the water behind it, and Score could see that the body was being dragged onto the shore on large seal-like flippers.

It struck again at Helaine, and once again she managed to make it halt before she could stab it with her sword. Then its tail whipped around, striking at her. She rolled to one side, but the tail caught her a glancing blow that sent her sprawling, obviously in pain.

And her sword was knocked from her hand, out of reach. Helaine groped for it, but it was too far away. And with her injured ankle, she couldn't dash for it. Roaring with impending victory, the monster struck down at her prostrate body.

And then the sword flew up from the ground and into Helaine's outstretched hand. Of course! She'd used her levitation power to get it back. As the mouth struck down at her, Helaine jabbed her sword in between the huge fangs. With a scream of pain, the monster reared back — tearing the sword from Helaine's grip, leaving it embedded in the thing's mouth.

Now Helaine was defenseless. She didn't have the time to grab her bow and arrows and use them. But Score and Pixel were on hand, and they ground to a halt beside her. Gasping for breath and ignoring the red spots dancing in front of his eyes, Score formed a large fireball, and sent it flying up at the monster's closest eye. He could see the evil creature glaring down at him.

The fireball exploded, and the thing screamed in pain. As Pixel tried to see what had happened, a flipper slammed into his legs. With a howl of pain, Pixel was flung back to the ground, all the breath knocked out of his body. Too dazed to act, he could only watch as Score attacked the beast. Score concentrated his powers through his emerald, causing the water around the creature to morph into ice.

The monster flexed its body, and shards of ice cracked and peeled away, showering the lake and water. One huge chunk slammed into Score, knocking him to his knees, shaken and confused.

Sensing victory at last, the monster's neck darted forward. For a terrible second, the only thing that Score could see was a mouthful of gigantic teeth heading toward him. And he had no way to stop it. . . .

There was a loud whistling sound, and suddenly the creature screamed in pain. Puzzled, Score could see two large spears sticking out of the monster's head. One had penetrated its blinded eye, and thick, icky liquid was dribbling from the site. The other had pierced the creature's snout. The monster reared up again, howling in anger and pain. The great tail lashed out, and then Helaine fired a couple of arrows at the beast's mouth.

Gradually Score's awareness returned, and he staggered upright, forming another fireball. He caught a blur of motion beside him, and some other creature hurried up. Another spear flew through the air and penetrated the neck of the monster. Someone had come to their aid! But he didn't have the time to see who it was right now. The thing in the lake was badly injured, but it was still terribly powerful. Score concentrated on his fireball, building it larger and larger, before he launched it directly at the open mouth of the monster.

The monster's head literally exploded into flames from the fireball. The spell had worked even better than he'd hoped! With one last scream, the monster died. Its huge body convulsed, and then slammed into the earth. The large neck and burning head barely missed him as the thing collapsed.

"Hot stuff," muttered Pixel weakly. He managed

a slight grin at Score, and then looked at Helaine. She seemed to be reasonably all right, but she wasn't looking back at them. She was staring past them, at the spear-throwers who had saved their lives. Score turned around to see who he had to thank.

There were three of them, standing there, snorting slightly and pawing the ground. They had the bodies of horses and the torsos and heads of people. Two of them were male, the third female. She and one of the males were a deep, midnight black in color, while the other male was milky white all over.

Centaurs!

CHAPTER 8

Helaine stared in fascination at the creatures that had just helped to save her life. She had always loved horses, and couldn't help but notice that the centaurs truly looked like horses merged with human beings. In the stories she'd heard, though, centaurs always had human coloring on their torsos and faces. These real centaurs were quite different — they were a uniform color all over. And, she saw, their hair became manes that extended down their human backs.

The female centaur wore some kind of covering across her torso, and all three wore bows and quivers across their shoulders. The two males had bags slung around the place where the horse half met the human half.

The dark centaur male stepped forward. Helaine saw that he had hooves just like a horse, and a slender, powerful body. "I am Dethrin," he said solemnly. "This is my sister, Amaris, and my comrade, Rothar."

Helaine struggled to her feet, and nodded. Both Score and Pixel seemed to have been struck speechless, staring at the magnificent creatures that had helped them. "I am Renald," Helaine said, using her alias. She had learned the trouble that came from giving out your true name on any world of the Diadem. "This is Score and Pixel. Thank you for your help."

"We weren't going to help," Rothar said, scowling slightly in Dethrin's direction. Helaine had a chilling feeling that Rothar would have preferred to let them die.

"We have a . . . policy of noninterference with humans," explained Dethrin, with an easy smile. "We leave them alone, and hopefully they leave us alone. It generally works."

"So why did you break it?" Helaine asked. She found herself liking this beautiful centaur. Maybe it was a mistake to do so, since she barely knew him, but he certainly *seemed* like a nice person.

Amaris gestured at the dead monster. "Serpent

steaks," she said with a wide grin. "My brother *adores* serpent steaks."

"Then," said Helaine drily, "by all means stay for dinner."

"I was hoping you'd say that." Dethrin nudged Rothar, who was still scowling. "Come on, you know you love a good serpent steak. And this one's half-cooked already."

Rothar glared at him darkly. "No good ever came from associating with humans, Dethrin. You, of all people, should know that."

"Calm down," Amaris advised. She crossed to where the two boys were standing, still silent and amazed. "Don't you two know how to talk?"

"Usually," Helaine replied, "it's hard getting them to shut up. I think they're in awe of you."

"Well, making steaks from this thing should cure them," said Dethrin with a laugh. He pulled a large knife from his pack, and headed for the dead monster. "Come on, you two. And you, Rothar. Let's get as much as we can and have a feast!"

Helaine watched the centaur take charge. Pixel and Score fell in to help, and soon started chatting with Dethrin, charmed by his easy manner. Amaris busied herself with making a fire. Helaine struggled to stand up, but couldn't take the pain in her ankle, and was forced to sit back again. "Sorry I'm no help," she apologized.

The centaurette paused in her work. "Injured your hoof?" she asked, sympathetically. "Well, as soon as I've got this fire going nice and hot, I'll see what I can do. I know a few herbs and poultices that might help here." She smiled. "It's not magic, but almost as good."

Helaine settled down to wait. Despite the fact that she liked their new companions, she kept her Book of Magic hidden. There was no sense in advertising their possessions, especially since they couldn't be certain that the centaurs were actually what they seemed.

After about a quarter of an hour, Amaris left the blazing fire and came over to Helaine. She'd prepared a pasty mix of herbs wrapped in a large, long purple leaf. "This might feel a little warm to you," she cautioned. "But that means it's doing its job. With luck, and if I've got my human anatomy right, you should be as good as new in the morning."

As the leaf was wrapped about her injured ankle, Helaine felt the heat begin almost immediately. It felt rather nice, in fact. "Thank you," she said. "I'm sure it'll be a great help."

Then the others arrived with huge chunks of serpent meat. Amaris took charge of setting the meat to cook, generally on large, flat stones she had found and placed into the fire. Then she ordered the males off to get washed in the lake. "No excuses," she cautioned. "You've killed the serpent, so it's safe."

"Aren't there likely to be more there?" asked Helaine. "After all, they have to breed."

"Yes," agreed Amaris. "But only one at a time gets to that size. The others are a lot smaller, and generally won't attack a person. One of those will now become the dominant serpent and start growing. In a few weeks, there will be another monster like that one."

"Sounds rough."

Amaris shrugged. "It means a constant supply of food for us if we can catch them. That's not usually possible with less than about thirty of us attacking them, so we don't have these steaks very often. No offense, but if you hadn't looked like you could beat this thing, we probably wouldn't have helped. Human visitors to Rawn generally haven't been very friendly to the centaurs."

"I can't imagine why," Helaine replied honestly.

"Maybe it's a lack of imagination on your part," Amaris suggested, with darker tones. "Ah, here's everyone back now." The other centaurs, Pixel and Score, washed and a little tidier, returned. "Well, it'll be a while before we eat, so why don't we get to know one another?"

"My sister, the hostess," joked Dethrin. "Well, it's a good idea." He settled down close beside Helaine. Flicking his tail occasionally, he gave her a grin. The others sat down with them. "So — what are you doing on Rawn, anyway?" Dethrin asked.

Helaine explained some of their story, with additions from Score and Pixel. The two boys seemed to have recovered from their awe of the centaurs and joined in the story of how they had been snatched from their own worlds, dragged to Treen, and almost killed by the magician Aranak. Though they mentioned their abilities to do magic, they all carefully avoided explaining about their gems. They finished by explaining how they had had run-ins with goblins and trolls, and finally the serpent.

"We saw some of that," Dethrin informed them. Seeing their surprise, he added, "We've been following you for almost a day now. You have to understand, humans are generally trouble here on Rawn. We wanted to make sure you weren't going to be. Most humans who come here are powerful magic-users. They either come to try to rule this world, or else to move on to the Inner Circuit of the Diadem. Most magic-users are ruthless, egotistical, and generally unpleasant. They have power, and want to either use it or else to rule the world."

"Which is why we avoid them," Rothar added darkly.

"Can't say I blame you," Pixel replied. "Humans sound pretty wretched to me, too. But we're not like that."

"No," Rothar growled. "They never are. At first."

"So there are no humans on Rawn?" asked Helaine, feeling slightly disappointed, but also a little glad. They didn't need another Aranak!

"There are one or two," Amaris replied. "But they tend to live a long way away from the centaurs. There's only one that's reasonably close. Her name is Shanara."

"Is she a magician?" asked Score.

"Of course." Dethrin looked surprised. "If she weren't, she'd be dead by now. She's known as the Magician of Shapes. Her biggest power is the ability to take on any form she chooses." He shrugged. "She can turn herself into anyone or anything. That way, she can stay hidden from any foes."

Helaine shuddered. "So anyone we meet might be her in disguise?" she asked.

"Or anything," agreed Dethrin cheerfully. "Even one of us. Or one of you."

Score shook his head. "I think we'd know it if she tried to impersonate one of us," he objected. "She might be able to *look* like one of us, but she'd never be able to *act* like one of us."

"Don't be so sure," Amaris cautioned him. "She's *very* good at what she does. And if she's got any reason to dislike you, all she needs to do is wait till one of you is alone and then replace that person. Trust me, you'd not be able to tell them apart."

"Wonderful," Score said glumly. "It sounds like paranoia time. How do you cope?"

Dethrin shrugged. "We can't do anything about it, so we don't. Generally, she leaves us alone, so we don't much care."

"Personally," Rothar added, "I'd like to see her destroyed. She's too dangerous to have around." He gave the trio a long, hard stare. "Hmmm . . . maybe with your combined powers you could take her on and defeat her for us?"

Amaris snorted. "And then we'd have *three* of them to worry about instead of just one," she pointed out. "Smart move!"

Rothar looked uncomfortable, and Dethrin gave a barking laugh. "I rather think he thought he could then kill these three humans once they'd disposed of Shanara for us," he exclaimed.

"The only good human is a dead human," Rothar said surlily.

"Well," Score commented, obviously angry,

"*we're* not the prejudiced ones here. Anyway, there's no way we would have done what you wanted anyway. We won't kill anyone for you."

Puzzled, Amaris asked, "But didn't you kill Aranak?"

"Yes," Helaine said. "But he left us no choice. He was trying too hard to kill us. We had to kill him before he succeeded." She grimaced. "And I still don't feel happy about it."

"And what about the goblins and trolls?" Amaris insisted. "Does that mean you only kill non-humans without worrying?"

"No," Pixel said hotly. "We didn't kill any of them. We just put them out of action so we could escape. We only kill things if we're attacked and there's no other option." He gestured at the bulk of the lake monster. "Like that thing."

"But we do hunt animals for food," Helaine said, feeling compelled to be honest. "Apart from that, we've no desire to hurt anything or anyone."

"And even less desire for power," Score added. "Look, we didn't ask to be kidnapped by the Beastials. We didn't ask to be sent through this maze of alien worlds. We didn't ask to have magical powers. These were all forced on us. All we want to do is to survive, and try to find some way off this planet." He glowered at Rothar. "As far as we're concerned, we'd be happy to leave you in peace — just as soon as we know how."

Amaris and Dethrin exchanged glances. "Then your best bet would be to seek out the wizard Shanara," Dethrin replied. "If there's a way off this planet, she'll know."

"But we *can't* if she can change her shape and look like anyone," Helaine objected.

"Sure we can," Pixel contradicted her. "You're forgetting magic again." He pulled out his ruby.

Amaris's eyes shone as she saw the gem, and she leaned toward it. "Sparklies," she murmured. "I *love* sparklies."

Her brother laughed. "That's always been one of her weaknesses," he informed them. "She'll do just about anything for jewelry."

"We could do with more ourselves," Pixel admitted. "We've discovered that they enhance our powers."

Helaine winced at this; did he *have* to tell the centaurs everything? He had to learn to keep his mouth shut sometimes!

Pixel held up the ruby. "This enables me to find anything. And, I hope, anyone."

Amaris sighed. "Why don't you use it to discover where more jewels are?" she suggested. "Then we could share them . . ."

Dethrin laughed again, and nudged her with his forehoof. "Amaris, restrain yourself. These humans don't owe you anything."

"Yes we do," Pixel answered. "The three of you helped save our lives. And I am kind of keen to see if there are any more jewels close by." He focused on the ruby, and instantly a beam of light flashed from it, burning through the sky to point at one of the mountains.

"That figures," Score said. "It's got to be the goblins, right?"

"Thgir," Pixel agreed, concentrating on what the ruby allowed him to see. "Ev'yeht tog siht elbidercni moor dellif htiw erom sepyt fo smeg naht I nac neve sseug. D'ew eb elba ot teg gnihtyna ew tnaw morf ereht."

"What?" Score asked.

Pixel put down the jewel and explained that the goblins had a special room filled with jewels.

"We can sneak in and take what we want," Score said. "Or use our sapphire to call the gems to us."

"No," said Helaine, very firmly. Everyone looked at her in surprise. "We're not thieves," she insisted. "Those aren't our gems, and we can't just take them. They belong to the goblins."

"Who attacked us without provocation," Score said hotly. "I figure they owe us! And, anyway, I happen to be a thief."

"Not while you're with us," Helaine insisted. "We can't steal from the goblins; it wouldn't be right."

"She's right, Score," Pixel agreed. "Much as I want those gems, it's not right to use our powers to steal from anyone. Even goblins. If we really want some gems, we'll have to figure out some way to trade for them."

"With *goblins*?" Score scoffed. "No way will they agree."

"Then we'll have to find some elsewhere," Helaine said. She gestured at Rothar. "The folk of this world already have a bad enough opinion of humans as it is. Do you want to add to that distrust?"

"I suppose not," Score said, sighing. "But you're taking a lot of the fun out of my life."

"You'll live," Pixel replied, grinning. "Now, let's see about finding Shanara, shall we?" Everyone leaned forward to watch as he concentrated on the ruby.

And nothing happened.

He shook his head, and settled back. "It's no good," he finally said. "I can't find any trace of her. I don't understand it."

Helaine shrugged. "She's a wizard," she answered. "She can either hide from us, or she's disguised, perhaps. Either way, I'm not too surprised you can't find her."

"Try looking for more Pages instead," Score suggested. "There might be some of them on this world. I had a dream last night that there was one here, held by someone who shifted shapes. And we've just discovered that Shanara can change shapes. Maybe, if we have more of the Pages, we can start getting some sense out of them."

Helaine winced; didn't either of the boys know to keep their mouths shut about *any* of their secrets?

"Yako." Pixel concentrated, and this time a bright beam of light shone out, past the goblin mountains. "I nac ees emos tros fo eltsac," Pixel informed them. "S'ti etiuq ecin, yllaer. S'ereht a moor htiw a gib nordluac, dna stol fo skoob. Tros fo yditnu, srepap lla vero a egral ksed. S'ereht emos dnik fo lamina ereht, oot. Hsidder ruf, gnol liat, gnipeels. On, s'ti nekow pu dna —" He looked startled, and the beam of light went out. "Ti did gnihtemos!" he exclaimed. Then he put the ruby down. "The animal did something that cut me off completely. Weird."

"But you got the location, right?" Score asked eagerly.

"Yes." Pixel nodded toward the mountains. "The castle's just past the goblins."

"So it looks like we're heading in that direction," Helaine said. She turned to Dethrin. "I don't know what your plans are, but we'll understand if you want to go your own way now."

"What?" Amaris exclaimed. "When there's a possibility of sparklies?"

Dethrin laughed. "It looks as though you may be stuck with us for a while," he said. "Does that disturb you?"

Helaine considered it. "No," she admitted honestly. She couldn't help liking the centaurs. Well, two of them at any rate. She couldn't trust Rothar, though. He was too obviously against them. "I think we'd enjoy your company." She gestured to her foot. "Though I'm not really going anywhere for a while."

"Fine," Dethrin replied. "That'll give us the chance to rest a bit, and to prepare some meat. Speaking of which, I hope the first steaks are done; my mouth is watering."

After lunch, they all decided to take it easy for the remainder of the day. With six of them now, it would be simple to split watches overnight and allow everyone to get plenty of sleep. Helaine felt herself relaxing for the first time in days.

The centaurs had recovered their spears from the serpent's carcass, and Dethrin returned Helaine's sword to her. Happily, she cleaned the blood and gore from it, and then resheathed it. She felt more naked without her weapon than she would have felt without her clothes. Magic was all well and good, but nothing made her feel safer than wearing her blade.

The males all went back to carving as much usable meat as possible from the serpent, while Amaris and Helaine conferred about moving their camp for the night. "That carcass will attract all kind of predators come nightfall," Amaris explained. "There's no sense in asking for trouble, so we'll just move around the lake a bit and set up another camp."

Helaine still found herself reluctant to talk about her powers. Then she realized that the centaurs had been following them earlier, so they had to know she was able to levitate. "I'll keep up," she promised. "But I won't be much use in carrying supplies."

"So rest," Amaris advised her. "There are plenty of us to do the work."

Together, they all started out for another site. Rothar had scouted around and found a good place, close to the river that Score and Pixel had been about to explore before the serpent attack. It took them about half an hour to reach it and start setting up camp again. They were beside the river, some thirty feet across, and with a rock wall to their backs some forty feet high. As they were building a fire for the evening, a frustratingly familiar voice made Helaine jump.

> "A quiet time, a little rest
> Will help you all withstand the test."

She whirled around to see Oracle standing there, clad in black as always, with an infuriating grin on his face. "Don't you *ever* have any good news for us?" she grumbled.

"More humans!" Rothar snarled, rearing slightly. "What did I tell you? Allow one in, and more follow."

"He's not exactly human," Pixel answered. "And we can't really control when he pops in and out. He usually turns up to warn us about something."

"Interesting," said Amaris. She abruptly stuck out a hand at Oracle. Everyone gasped when her hand went right through his body. "Some kind of a projection."

"He *isn't* real," Score said. "I knew it."

"Only you neglected to mention it," Helaine scoffed. She scowled at Oracle. "If this is just a projection, are you standing somewhere else and sending it to us?"

> "No, young lady, don't forget
> What you see is what you get.
> This semblance of life is all of me
> All I was, or e'er will be."

111

Oracle looked almost sad at this statement.

"You're not a ghost, or something?" asked Pixel, obviously disturbed by the thought.

> "What I am is what I am
> I am no ghost or living man."

"This is getting us nowhere," Score grumbled. "Okay, why are you here this time?"

Oracle cheered up slightly. Helaine knew that this meant he had bad news to deliver.

> "The wizard here is now your foe
> Yet to her castle you must go.
> Trust nothing that you think you see
> For anything live might well be she."

"That's a big help," Score said. "We were planning to visit her anyway. But why should we believe you that she's got it in for us?"

> "The trolls attacked because she employed
> An illusion of their homes destroyed."

"Well, that explains that," Helaine commented. "She set the trolls onto us, hoping they'd kill us."

"*If* you can believe this . . . thing," Amaris said, eyeing Oracle with great suspicion. "Is he a friend of yours?"

"Hardly that," Score answered. "I trust him about as far as I can throw him. And since I can't even touch him, that's not very far at all."

Oracle shrugged.

"My warnings are meant for your own good
But only if they're understood."

And then he vanished.

"Well," Score said with some satisfaction, "I'm glad he's gone again. He really irritates me."

"I don't trust him," Amaris said firmly.

"Nor do I," Score agreed. The two of them seemed to be getting along well.

"But his warnings are often accurate," Helaine pointed out. "So I'm inclined to agree that we should be very careful about this Shanara. Whether he's telling the truth or not, we have no reason to trust her, either. Remember that Aranak claimed to be our friend, and wasn't." She glanced at Dethrin. "And you yourselves said that any humans who live on Rawn are either power-mad or greedy."

"I agree," Dethrin said with a nod. "You would be foolish not to assume that Shanara is your enemy."

"Wonderful," Rothar snapped. "We're hooking up with three humans that already have a wizard against them. No good will come of this, you mark my words."

CHAPTER 9

In the morning, Pixel looked around the camp with suspicion. The three centaurs and his companions were up and about, getting ready for departure. But he couldn't get out of his mind the possibility that one of them was Shanara in disguise. She could easily have replaced whoever was on watch, for example. Or if anyone left the party for any reason, who could say if it was that person who came back — or whether it was Shanara in their guise? He shuddered at the uncertainty.

It was some relief to discover that Helaine felt a great deal better. He couldn't help worrying about her, even knowing that she was tougher than he was. The poultice that Amaris had applied to the girl's ankle had taken down the swelling completely, and Helaine was delighting in being able to walk on it again. Unless, of course, this was Shanara, pretending to be Helaine. In which case, her foot would have been fine, wouldn't it? Pixel realized that he was starting to get paranoid, and he deliberately worked at cheering up. Only Rothar appeared to be in a sour mood as they struck camp and started for the mountain that Pixel's ruby indicated held the horde of gems that they would probably need.

On the way, Rothar insisted on being the scout, and headed out on his own. Pixel knew that this was because the centaur still didn't trust any humans, and didn't want to be around them at all if he could avoid it. Pixel wished the centaur would understand that they weren't enemies, but there didn't seem to be much chance of that. And, with him gone, the travelers could talk and relax a little. But how could they know that he *was* Rothar when he came back?

Or maybe he was *already* Shanara, and had gone off to set up a trap for them?

"Maybe you could explain a few things to us," Pixel asked Dethrin. "We're still trying to figure out why we were kidnapped in the first place, and what's going on in the Diadem. We keep finding references to the Triad. Do you know anything about them?"

Dethrin shrugged. "There are plenty of stories, of course, but that's probably all they are: stories. Basically, the heart of the Diadem is a world that's off-limits to all but the most powerful magicians. Nobody knows what happens there, but it's supposed to be the heart of the magic. The Three Who Rule are despots, tyrants who rule there jointly because together they have great power."

Score raised an eyebrow. "Three together stronger than individually? That sounds awfully familiar. And there are Three Who Rule and three of us. Can that be a coincidence?"

"There's no coincidence in magic," Amaris told him. "Things are the way they are for a reason. For example, if you want to have power over something, you need to know three things."

"The true name, the form, and the substance," Score said. "Yes, we've heard that before."

"Right," agreed Amaris, with a slight smile. "Now, nobody knows the true names of the Three, of course. They're not stupid enough to allow those out. But the form is obvious — there are three of them. Two male, one female, just like the three of you. Again, that can't be a coincidence."

"What are you getting at?" asked Pixel, puzzled.

"I'm not a magic-user, obviously," Amaris replied. "None of us magical creatures can use the magic that shapes us. But it seems to me that somebody might be trying to use the three of you as a weapon against the Three Who Rule. You do seem to have very strong innate magical abilities, and someone is going to a good deal of trouble to make sure you learn how to use them: those Pages you seem to be getting, and the messages that are left for you. I think it's possible that you're being manipulated into a fight with the Three."

Pixel felt very uneasy at the thought. "But we don't want to fight anyone," he objected.

"You may not have a lot of choice," Dethrin said. "This unknown foe of yours is leading you on the way he, she, or it wants you to go. It seems to me that there are two different forces at work here — one trying to help you, one trying to hinder or kill you."

"So we're caught up in the middle of someone else's battle?" Helaine asked grimly. "It does make sense — and I don't like it one bit."

"Yes," agreed Pixel slowly. "And not only that . . . If we *are* being trained as a weapon, then it's not going to be easy to discover which side we *should* be on. The person helping us may be doing it so that we can kill the Three Who Rule, and that may be because they're tyrants who need replacing. Or because the person helping us wants to take their place."

"Or," Amaris added, "they could be fighting

among themselves. According to some stories, they don't get along with each other very well, and they are always arguing. It's possible that they're having some kind of war."

Pixel paused to consider this. "That would make sense," he agreed slowly. "The three of them together hold the magic of the Diadem in balance, right? And if they're fighting, the balance is gone. We know for a fact that some of our spells go wrong for no really good reason. Maybe it's because of in-fighting among the Three Who Rule, upsetting the balance of magic?"

Helaine looked impressed. "That's not a bad idea," she agreed. "It does make some sense of what's going on. And the other idea, that we're being trained as some sort of weapon against them, also makes sense."

"And it means that we'd better find a way to get out of this plot fast," Score said. "Unlike you, I don't like fighting at all. I don't want to get caught up in somebody else's battle, thank you very much."

Helaine nodded. "I agree. This is not our fight, and we are being used as pawns. In that circumstance, I don't want to fight, either. Maybe with these gems we're after, we can find a way off this world and out of the plans of whoever is doing all of this."

"Good luck," said Dethrin drily. "You'll probably

need to find Shanara for the way off Rawn, and you discovered last night that you can't do that."

"There are always possibilities," said Pixel. "We're still learning to use our powers and there's so much we don't know yet. Maybe with more gems we can figure out some other way to contact her."

"And then what?" Amaris asked. "She set the trolls onto you. Even now, she could be spying on you, and planning to kill you. Perhaps you should have some plan to kill her first, for your own protection."

"No!" Pixel exclaimed immediately. He was echoed by Helaine and Score. "We don't want to hurt anyone," he explained to the puzzled centaur. "If we can talk to her, maybe she'll realize that we're not her enemies."

Dethrin snorted. "She's a magician, my friend," he said. "That sort tend to be very powerful, very arrogant, and very stubborn. She may be afraid that you're here to kill her, whatever you claim, or she may just be jealous of your power. Either way, she's not likely to listen to you."

"We have to try to talk," said Pixel stubbornly. "If she doesn't listen . . . well . . . we'll have to see what happens."

Amaris gave a great sigh, and her body shivered. "Helaine," she begged, "you're a warrior. You understand the need to be prepared. Surely you can convince your friends that you have to have a weapon you can use against this magician? For your own protection?"

Helaine considered the point. "The problem with having a weapon," she answered, "is that it makes you a target. If we do have one, she may think we plan to use it whatever we say. That could cause us greater trouble than anything."

"And if you go in defenseless, she might just kill you without thinking," Amaris objected. "Look, I like you three. I don't want to see you get hurt."

"Trust me," said Score with a grin, "I don't want to see me get hurt, either. I can see your point, but . . ." He squirmed uncomfortably. "I just don't feel *right* using my powers to hurt anyone. Even people who are trying to kill us."

Pixel nodded. "One of the nice things about being able to use magic," he added, "is that there is often a way to use it without causing serious damage. Provided it works right."

Shaking her head, Amaris made her mane ripple in the sunlight. "I think you're being very foolish, but I hope you're right."

The journey continued. Pixel couldn't keep his black thoughts from resurfacing. Was one of them even now the disguised Shanara? Or was she waiting for them, laying another trap? Maybe she'd figured out that they were going after the gems, and would be waiting? He tried to shake the thoughts, because there was nothing he could do about them. They kept returning, and he constantly viewed his companions to see if he could detect anything odd about them that might expose them as fakes.

Rothar deigned to join them again when they stopped for lunch, but he avoided sitting too close to the humans, and he shot off scouting again as soon as the meal was over. Amaris caught Pixel's look at the vanishing centaur's back.

"Don't be too harsh on Rothar," she said gently. "His sister was killed by a magician six years ago. The magician thought that powdered centaur hooves were useful in an elixir of eternal life."

"Oh." Pixel started to realize that Rothar had very good reasons to distrust humans. "I'm sorry to hear that."

"And I'll bet that the powdered hooves didn't work, either," Score put in. "There are all kinds of stupid legends like that on Earth, too."

Dethrin shrugged. "Hard to say. The magician was killed by Shanara, so it certainly didn't do him much good. And it left Rothar very bitter."

"I don't blame him," Helaine said. "If a human had killed my sister, I'd be very bitter, too. I'll have to be a bit more considerate of his feelings."

Pixel nodded. It seemed that very little around here was straightforward. Even Rothar's prejudice had good cause. Pixel was about to start up again when he realized they had a visitor. "Heads up, guys," he said. "The long streak of misery is back."

Oracle laughed at this description, not at all offended. He gave a bow, and it was hard to tell if he was mocking them or not.

> "The path you're taking is the best
> To bring you to the perfect test."

"Oh, great," Score said, scowling. "He thinks this is a good idea. That means it's got to be a mistake."

"Or that he wants you to think it's a mistake," added Amaris, eyeing Oracle with a very bleak look. The illusion didn't seem to be concerned.

Helaine stepped forward. "Okay," she said. "Enough of your cryptic warnings. Tell me something straight. This Three Who Rule — are we going to have to fight them?"

Oracle raised an eyebrow, looking very surprised for once.

"The path you take is very clear,
And the Three you mention are all near.
To come to your appointed fate
You must face the Three — but wait!
Your first opponent is in this place
Wearing someone else's face.
It is her challenge you must pass
Or your quest will be doomed, alas."

Score groaned. "I really hate your silly rhymes," he complained. "And your veiled messages. So we *do* have to face the Three Who Rule? But first we have to go up against Shanara?"

"And she's around here somewhere in disguise?" added Helaine, equally irritated. "Just a simple yes or no would help. And how close to us is she? Is she with us? Or is she one of us?"

Oracle spread his hands.

"I have said all that shall be allowed
And danger does upon you crowd."

And then he vanished.

"I really wish he'd be a little bit more helpful," Score complained. He looked at the rest of them. "So, if we can believe him — Shanara's here, somewhere.

Maybe even one of you." He glanced at Amaris and Dethrin. "Maybe Rothar. Maybe even one of us."

"Right," agreed Pixel. "After all, we've all been alone for at least a few minutes today. Shanara could have taken the place of any one of us without a problem. And if she's as good at this disguise business as she's supposed to be, then there's no way we can tell which of us she is."

"If any," Dethrin pointed out. "You only have that Oracle's word that she's here at all. And if you can't trust him, he may be lying to you to keep you off-guard."

Pixel sighed. "I just wish, for once, that there was something nice and simple about this whole thing," he complained. Oracle's warning had left them with virtually nothing but mutual suspicion now. Was he telling the truth? Had Shanara replaced one of their number? And if so, who? Amaris? Rothar? Dethrin? Maybe even Score or Helaine?

Helaine *was* walking awfully easily on her injured ankle, after all. Was it *really* her? And how about Rothar? He hated humans, and he'd spent a lot of time away from them today. Shanara could have taken his place easily, and nobody would know. And he was the one scouting for danger ... If it was her instead ... "I just had a really bad thought," he announced. "What if Shanara has replaced Rothar? If there's trouble, she's not likely to let us know, is she? We could be walking right into an ambush, and we wouldn't know it."

Score nodded slowly. "Yes. Or *you* could be her, trying to make us paranoid." He shook his head. "Any of you could be her. I can't trust any of you now."

Helaine gave a strangled cry. "This is what she wants!" she exclaimed. "She's setting us against each other! She can only be one of us at the most! If we make joint decisions as to what to do, she can't hurt us. I think we should carry on the way we're going."

"*You* think," Score snapped. "But are you really you?"

Helaine looked as if she were about ready to punch out Score's lights — which was exactly how the real Helaine would behave. Or how a frustrated imposter might behave . . .

Pixel couldn't decide what to believe. The threat of a possible imposter in their group was too scary to want to believe. Surely things couldn't get worse than this?

At that moment, Rothar galloped out of the trees. "Goblins!" he exclaimed. "A whole army of them! They'll be here in a couple of minutes, and they seem to be really mad."

CHAPTER 10

Score groaned. It looked as though they were going to be in for a fight, no matter how much he, Pixel, and Helaine wanted to avoid one. It reminded him too much of what he had seen on the streets of New York. The street gangs there had fought constantly, using fists, knives, and even guns, and often for the stupidest of reasons. People would be injured and killed over supposed slights that Score couldn't even understand. Some kind of macho posing, he supposed.

And it looked as if the goblins had this same philosophy. He and the others had done nothing to the goblins at all. Maybe a bit of minor trespassing, if the mountain where they had landed happened to belong to the goblins. But you don't kill someone just because they set foot on land you claim. And now the goblins were out for revenge over their last defeat.

"I hate this attitude," Score said. "Why won't they just leave us alone?"

"Goblins are like that," Dethrin replied. "They simply enjoy fighting. It doesn't have to make sense to them. The only way you'll stop them is to convince them that you're better fighters than they are. If you do, they'll leave you in peace."

"But to do that," added Amaris, "you're going to have to kill quite a lot of them."

"No," said Score and Pixel together. Score shrugged. "Okay, I'll admit I'm a coward, but I really don't like the idea of having the blood of an intelligent being on my hands. Or, in the case of the goblins, semi-intelligent. I've always preferred to avoid fights, given the chance."

Rothar snorted in disgust. "Well, you won't be able to avoid this one." He had his spear at the ready, slotted through the restraint on his pack where he could grab it when needed. As he spoke, he unslung his bow and nocked an arrow. "They will be here in moments. Either fight or die."

"That's the trouble with this whole setup!" Score exclaimed. His temper had finally frayed through. "It's always doing what other people want! Not what I want. Well, I don't want to hurt even the stupid goblins."

"There's no other option," Amaris insisted.

"There are *always* options," Helaine replied. She looked at Score, and he felt a puzzled thrill. There was almost respect in her look. "What did you have in mind?"

"Our one big advantage — magic." He took his emerald from his pocket. "Let's not fight this on their terms. It's about time we kicked some serious butt here."

"I'm not entirely sure what that means," Helaine answered with a grin, removing her sapphire. "But I think I get the attitude."

"Sit this one out," Score advised the centaurs. "But . . . well . . . be ready, just in case."

"As you wish," Dethrin said, bowing slightly. Rothar looked as if he were about to object, but Dethrin made a chopping motion with his hand. "No! For the moment, we shall allow them to fight this their way." Sullenly, Rothar subsided, but kept his bow at the ready. Amaris and Dethrin both strung their own, and waited.

The goblins, as always, advertised their advance with howls and screams of delight as they anticipated a fight — or, more likely, a massacre. They had to be pretty angry to come out in the daylight like this, and from the sound of it there were a lot more than there had been in the battle of the cave.

"Get dyrea," Score said as he clutched his emerald. The emerald made him say *syllables* in reverse! This could be awkward. His hand was sticky with sweat, and his insides were churning. He *really* hated fighting. It wasn't simply the thought of getting hurt that bothered him. He didn't like to hurt back, either. So he *really* hoped his idea would work, and they wouldn't have to kill anyone.

The first wave of goblins, howling and brandishing clubs, scythes, and pikes, broke through the trees. The ugly little runts grinned and screamed insults when they saw their foes waiting for them. They obviously anticipated an easy victory, because there had to be hundreds of the little beasts.

Well, they were in for a shock. Using his emerald, Score began his transformations. First he exploded several trees into blazing pillars of fire. That produced howls of shock and some pain, as the clothing of several of the goblins caught fire, and the victims rolled on the floor to put out the flames. This made other goblins trip over them, fall, and then start punching whichever poor unfortunate they had stumbled over.

Grinning now, Score opened a pit in front of the leaders of the goblins. As the ground turned to laughing gas, the goblins collapsed, yelling, into the hole —

and then started to giggle uncontrollably. Way to go! They couldn't fight for rolling on the floor laughing. This worked so well that Score simply started creating clouds of laughing gas around groups of goblins. Those affected dropped their weapons and collapsed, laughing and giggling, totally useless in the fight.

But he couldn't stop everyone. Some got through because there were simply so many in the goblin army. Helaine turned on the others with her power of levitation. Goblins suddenly left the ground like rockets heading for the moon. They flew up into the tallest trees, where the lucky ones managed to grab branches and hang on for dear life. The less fortunate ones went sailing up, arms and legs windmilling uselessly. Pixel, determined not to be left out, was firing off balls of fire like fireworks around the goblins.

It wasn't so much a fight as a disaster. The goblins couldn't make any kind of leeway against the three of them. No matter how many attacked, Score, Pixel, and Helaine kept them laughing, flying, or falling. Behind, Score could hear Amaris and Dethrin laughing. He could almost hear Rothar scowling furiously.

There was absolutely no question that this had to be the stupidest fight ever held. All it needed was. . . . Well, why not? Score was starting to enjoy this, so he materialized custard pies right in the paths of several goblins, who ran slap into them, and stood there, shocked, custard and pieces of crusts dripping from their faces.

"Food fight!" Score howled happily. He started to materialize all sorts of food that he could think of. The startled goblins were pelted with Jell-O, peanut butter, hot gravy, fried chicken . . . anything and everything that Score happened to think of. Several were left spluttering in muddy holes when, instead of turning the soil into gas, he turned it into cola instead.

The force of the goblin army slowed and then finally halted. Too many were laughing, flying, or cleaning food off themselves to be able to fight. Their mood of battle-lust was broken, and they were more puzzled than anything else. Helaine continued to toss goblins into the air, but slowed down as the attack ground to a halt. She still had over forty goblins spinning helplessly about sixty feet from the ground. Pixel tossed less and less fireballs.

Suddenly, a large shadow came across the ground from behind. Startled, Score whirled around, thinking it was another goblin attack, but realized instantly that he was wrong.

It was a huge bird, with a wingspan of over forty feet. It had the claws and beak of an eagle, but was far too large to be any kind of bird Score had ever known.

"A roc!" Amaris exclaimed.

The huge, flesh-eating creature rocketed down on the helpless goblins floating in mid-air. It was going after prey that couldn't escape!

"Let them down, fast!" Score cried to Helaine. "Or they'll be roc-food!"

She hastily complied, dropping the goblins back down to earth safely, but with serious motion sickness. Several of them immediately started heaving up their last meal.

The roc screamed in frustration at losing its prey, and banked overhead. It was still intent on grabbing as many goblins for lunch as it could manage, and dived down toward the forest below. Score realized that by his torching the trees he had created a clearing, allowing the bird plenty of space to pluck at the goblins on the ground. The goblins, meanwhile, scattered in terror, falling over one another in their haste to escape the slashing claws and talons.

"Lk t!" Helaine snapped, focusing through her gem.

At the last second it was as if a huge, invisible hand had whirled out of nowhere and slapped the roc really hard. Stunned, the bird tumbled backward through the air, its wings beating frantically as it tried to right itself and attack the goblins again. But Helaine now had her levitation working on it, and no matter how hard it tried, the roc couldn't return to the attack. It beat its wings uselessly as it tried, and harsh screams of rage came from the creature's throat. But none of it made any difference. Finally, frustrated and confused, it turned and flew off, seeking easier prey.

Amaris stared at the three humans, puzzled. "You saved the goblins," she said. "You should have let the roc eat them. That would have discouraged them and probably ended the fight."

"How many times do we have to tell you that we don't want anybody to die?" growled Score. The centaurette was proving to be very slow to understand.

"Do you think this will endear you to the goblins?" jeered Rothar. "Think again. They're not known for their gratitude."

"I didn't do it for them," Helaine informed him. "I did it for *me*. I don't like to see anyone suffer or die. Not even a goblin. And if they're not grateful — tough. I don't care. We did what was right."

Score and Pixel nodded, and Score could see that the centaurs were having trouble understanding their attitude. That was nothing compared to what the goblins were going through. As Score watched, one of the goblins, who was taller and heavier-set than most, spoke to his companions and then threw down his scythe and slowly walked toward the humans, his hands held out to show they were empty. His ugly face was filled with confusion. Halting about ten feet away, he looked from one to the other, and then at the centaurs.

"We do not understand," he said, finally. "You stopped the roc. Why?"

"Let me handle this," Score said quickly, before Helaine could open her mouth and take charge as she always did. "This is something I understand, okay?" To his surprise, the girl didn't complain or argue. She simply nodded, and settled back. Hoping he had been telling the truth, Score stepped forward.

"We respect the goblins," he said. "You are all very good fighters. Too good for us, in fact. We couldn't allow such noble foes to be so unfairly slaughtered."

The goblin leader preened himself at this. Score had suspected he would. As he had guessed, it was just another macho contest, and he knew how to avoid losing those. You changed the rules.

"Goblins are the best fighters there are," the leader agreed.

"Right," Score answered. "That's why we had to cheat to stop you. We knew that if we fought you with swords and spears, you'd have wiped the floor with us."

"True," agreed the goblin, grinning. "You'd have been mincemeat."

"We knew that," Score replied. "So we had to stop you with things you couldn't beat. Gases, pits, and flying lessons. We could never have beaten you in a fair fight."

The goblin leader seemed to be almost happy now. He scratched his hairy body and nodded cheerily. "Too true," he agreed. Then he scowled. "But why didn't you kill us? We would have killed you."

"Yes, I know," Score agreed. "But we don't want to be enemies of the goblins. We respect you too much. We admire your fighting skills, and your ability to work. We want to be allies with you."

"Allies with us?" The leader was way beyond puzzled now. "Nobody wants to be allies with goblins."

"Well, *we* do," Score said. "We admire you. We don't attack you — not that we could win if we did! — and we help you. In return, you don't attack us, and you help us. That way, we all win, and we get to admire your skills without getting killed."

The goblin leader thought this idea over a bit. It was obviously something that had never occurred to him before. His brain wasn't exactly king-sized, and he was on new ground with his thoughts. Score could see the conflicting emotions playing over his face as he thought hard. But eventually he grinned.

"Sounds good to me," the leader said. "We'll make you all honorary goblins, and that should solve it. Then we can tell you all about our skills, and show you what we can do. Maybe we could even pick a fight together, eh?" He grinned widely, and flopped a hairy arm around Score's shoulders. "Maybe against those stuck-up centaurs, hey?"

"Not them," Score said. "They're already our allies. Maybe we can find someone else to attack instead?"

"Okay," the leader agreed amicably. He turned back to face his army. "Okay, lads!" he called. "I've just declared these three humans honorary goblins. Nobody's to pick a fight with them, or he'll answer to me. And I'll rip his intestines out and strangle him with them. Got that?"

There was a chorus of slightly sullen agreement, as the goblins started picking themselves and their weapons up.

"Right," the leader said, turning back to Score. "They'll behave, because they know I'll do what I said if they don't. So, you folks feel like coming back for a feast? We always have a good munch after we win a battle."

Score decided not to point out that the goblins had actually lost one. After all, he, Pixel, and Helaine were now honorary goblins, and *they* had won . . . so maybe, in a way, the goblins had won after all. "Sounds great to me," he agreed. "Then we can talk

over a few ideas we've got, and maybe try out our mutual cooperation."

"Sure thing," agreed the leader happily. "For
starters . . . do you think you could make some more
of that strange liquid you put in your traps? I had a
couple of mouthfuls, and it was absolutely heavenly!"

Grinning, Score nodded. It looked as if their al-
liance was going to be cemented because he could
create soda pop. Magic had its uses, after all.

CHAPTER 11

Despite her initial skepticism, Helaine discovered that the goblins actually did know how to throw a party. Since their leader had declared the humans (and, more reluctantly, the three centaurs), their friends, the attitude of the goblins toward them had totally changed. All in all, the party was a lot of fun. Only Rothar refused to unbend and enjoy himself. He ate and drank with the rest of them, but there was always that emotional wall between him and the humans. After what he had suffered, she could hardly blame him for hating humans.

"So," Helaine finally said, unable to eat or drink

anything more, "it is definitely good being a friend of the goblins."

"Naturally." The leader, whose name was Gunther, belched loudly. "We're the best cooks anywhere, as well as the best fighters."

Realizing that a belch was a compliment to the food, Helaine managed a fairly respectable one of her own that met with Gunther's beaming approval. "We make a good team," she added. "There's something you can do for us, and we hope that there's something we can do in return for you."

"Sounds good," agreed Gunther. "Allies do that sort of thing, I believe. So — what can we do for you?"

"Well," Helaine explained, "as you know, we're magic-users. We've discovered that if we use gemstones, they amplify our powers. We've got a few gems, but we really need more to be able to use all of our abilities properly."

Gunther nodded. "And we goblins are the best gem miners in the universe," he said proudly. "Whatever you need, I'm sure we have." His eyes narrowed. "But you have magical powers," he said slowly. "Surely you can just take from us what you need, whether we want to give them or not."

"We could," agreed Helaine. "But we wouldn't treat our allies like that."

"Then I'll see if I can come up with a favor you can do for us in return." He staggered to his feet. "I'll have a few words with my chiefs and get back to you on it."

Turning back to her companions, Helaine smiled. "We may be on our way to a deal," she announced. *If the goblins are serious about being our allies,* she added mentally. They might be setting up a trap instead.

"I have to confess," Dethrin said, "that you have impressed me. I've never heard of anyone actually making friends with goblins before. You three seem to have some rare talents."

"Thanks," Pixel said. "Now, once we get those gems, we have to find our way to Shanara's palace. All I know is that it's around these mountains somewhere."

One of the goblin women stopped, and wrinkled her nose. "Shanara's palace?" she echoed. "You're looking for that place?"

Pixel sat forward eagerly. "Yes," he agreed. "You know where it is?"

"Of course I do," she replied. "Every goblin knows that. We'd have to be idiots or blind not to — no offense meant, of course."

"None taken," Helaine replied with a laugh. "So we could get a guide to take us there?"

"Sure," the goblin woman replied. "Just ask anyone." She refilled the goblets with more of the cola Score had made, and went on her way.

"Well," Score said, surprised and pleased, "that part of things looks like it's easier than any of us expected. So all we need to do now is to see what the goblins want in exchange for the jewels. Then we can be on our way."

Rothar snorted. "Do you think this Shanara will simply allow you to walk into her palace?" he asked scornfully. "She is a magician, and a human. She will kill you when you even *try*."

"She'll try to kill us, maybe," Helaine agreed. "But, as you've seen, we're tougher to kill than we appear to be. I'm sure we'll think of something."

"Idiots," muttered the centaur. But he subsided and returned to his food.

Gunther strode across the room and plopped himself down in his seat again. Taking a huge helping of food, he started to munch, and then talk around his mouthful. "Okay," he said, "we've decided. We have a problem we've not been able to solve, so we figure that you might be able to help us. If you can, we'll let you loose in our treasure vault, and you can help yourselves to whatever you want."

"Sparklies," murmured Amaris, happily.

"Sounds good," agreed Helaine. "So, what's the favor we can do for you?"

Gunther shook his head. "It's not simple," he warned her. "It could be very dangerous indeed. If you don't feel like doing it, we'll understand, and we'll still be allies." He chewed on his lower lip for a moment before continuing. "In the heart of the mountain, there lives a wyrm. We want it killed."

"A worm?" asked Score, shaking his head. "Hey, there must be millions of worms inside this place. How are we going to find just one?"

"Not an earthworm," Gunther explained patiently. "A wyrm. It is a monstrous creature, akin to a snake, only much larger. It lives within its own tunnels, and comes out from time to time to eat. It eats goblins. So, we should like it killed. We've gone after it ourselves, but none who has sought it out has ever returned." He shrugged. "As I said, it's very dangerous, so I'll understand if you say no."

Helaine leaned forward. "As your allies, we'll help." She just hoped this wasn't the goblin's way of getting rid of unwanted guests. She tapped the hilt of her sword. "We will go after it." She glanced at Pixel and Score, who both looked rather worried. She didn't feel the contempt that she once had for their abilities, but they were not warriors. "Perhaps I'd better go alone."

"No," Pixel protested. Score echoed this, after a moment's hesitation. Helaine knew that neither really wanted to go along, but they wouldn't simply abandon her. She felt . . . almost a bond of affection for both of them. Scared as they were, they were willing to stick by her.

"It might be better for me to go alone," she said gently. "In these tunnels, we'd only get in one another's way. I'm better off on my own."

"Not on your own," Gunther said firmly. "If the centaurs are our friends, too, then one of them should go with you."

"Right," agreed Dethrin, eagerly. "I'll do it." He grinned down at Helaine.

Fighting down the feeling of affection she felt toward him, Helaine shook her head. "No," she said, a trifle sadly. "I'm sorry, Dethrin, but I can't trust you. It's nothing personal. But remember what Oracle said — that Shanara is close to us, in disguise. It could be you. I don't want to have you with me and not be able to trust you implicitly to do the right thing if we hit trouble."

"Then take me instead," Amaris said.

"Same problem," Helaine answered. "Look, I like you both, but I don't *know* that you're who you say you are." She looked grim. "I'll take Rothar."

"Rothar?!" There was a chorus from everyone at the table.

"Are you crazy?" demanded Pixel. "He hates humans. You can't trust him at all."

"That's precisely why I *can* trust him," Helaine answered. To their blank stares, she explained: "Shanara, if she is one of us, is trying to spy on us and learn what she can. Rothar has spent as much time as he can as far away from us as possible. He's not been able to spy on us. Therefore, he's the more likely not to be Shanara in disguise. So he's the only one of you I can trust implicitly to be who he says he is, and to help me when I need it."

Rothar was actually smiling. "Beautifully logical," he said. "But what makes you believe you can trust me to keep my word if I accompany you? I could just stay back and let the wyrm kill you, you know."

"I don't think you'd do that," Helaine argued, a slight smile on her lips. "That would be a *human* thing to do, not a centaur action. You're a warrior, Rothar, just as I am. If you give your word, you'll keep it. So, I ask for it. Will you go with me and fight with me?"

The centaur stared at her with an unreadable expression. Helaine could only pray that she'd read his character right. She was almost certain she had. . . . But it was the *almost* that was causing her problems.

"Very well," he said, finally, and there was a collective sigh of relief around the table. He studied her grimly. "I could almost bring myself to like you — if you weren't human. You understand." He clambered

144

to his feet from where he had been sitting. "Shall we go?"

"Yes." Helaine felt a deep satisfaction. Whatever happened, there was no way that Rothar would abandon her. She turned to Gunther. "Take us to where the wyrm lives," she ordered.

It was a long walk, lasting almost an hour. They went deeper down the dark, rock-hewn tunnels, past more of the goblin side-tunnels, and through two more large caverns. Finally, Gunther and the goblins with him halted beside a narrow tunnel that led down at an angle. It was about six feet across, so there was room for both her and Rothar.

"You should let us come with you," Pixel said, obviously worried for her safety.

"No," she answered, oddly touched by his concern. But he was not equipped for this kind of a fight. "Stay here. I'll be back," she promised.

Score fidgeted uncomfortably. "I know we don't always agree," he said. "But, well, I respect you. Don't go and do anything dumb like getting killed, okay?"

"I'll try not to," Helaine answered, smiling slightly. She turned to Rothar. "Ready?"

"No," he answered. "But I will follow anyway." He held his spear in his hand. "Lead on."

Helaine nodded. She didn't look back as she took in her left hand the burning torch that Gunther had offered her. Drawing her sword, she stepped into the wyrm tunnel. Refusing to surrender to the worry that gripped her, she forced her feet to set off on the path downward.

The path was steep, but curiously smooth. The goblin passages had all been cut using picks and shovels, and had a rough-hewn look to them. This tunnel was completely smooth, and couldn't have been cut. So how did the wyrm create it? Still, it was easier to travel than the goblin's tunnels, and Helaine made good time. There was an odd smell in the air, faint but clear. She couldn't place it at all, but it seemed to grow stronger the further they went. It had to mean that they were getting closer to the wyrm.

"This place is very odd," Rothar commented. "And I see no signs of the goblins who are supposed to have come down here before us."

"Maybe they got further than this," suggested Helaine. Or, maybe, there hadn't really been any goblins, and this was a trap after all. She kept a firm grip on her sword. Like Rothar, she had a bad feeling about this expedition. But she wasn't going to turn back now. Aside from the humiliation it would cause her, the goblins needed her help. And she needed the jewels.

She could only hope that she and Rothar could deal with the wyrm when they found it. Rothar stayed behind her, speaking very little. He was clearly not too happy about being partnered with her, but she was certain she could rely on him when trouble came.

And then it came.

The tunnel tended to be mostly straight, as if whatever had cut it simply plowed ahead. Goblin tunnels followed natural flaws in the rocks, so they often wound about a lot as the goblins cut the veins in the easiest directions. The wyrm didn't bother with that. It went straight as an arrow wherever it wanted to go. However it cut the rock, it did so without any obvious regard to obstacles. The light from the torch Helaine carried didn't illuminate more than about twenty feet in front of them, so she almost stumbled into the wyrm's nest before she realized that they had reached their target.

It was a large cave-like shape in the rock, as smooth as the tunnels, and just as bare. It was about thirty feet across, and ten feet tall. And, curled in the middle of the open space, was the wyrm itself.

It was huge, at least twenty feet long, Helaine estimated. Since it was coiled, it was hard to be certain. It loomed like a monstrous snake. The head rose and pointed in their direction, and Helaine shuddered. It's red eyes were cold and deathly. The only other feature on the head was a large, circular mouth. This was slightly open, and Helaine saw rows of twisted teeth. The creature was a sickly green and looked absolutely disgusting. Its tail produced some kind of dark, slimy goo.

"Gods," muttered Rothar, obviously as appalled as she was. "What a nightmare."

"And there's still no sign of any goblins," Helaine murmured. "I think that creature must digest them whole. But how does it cut the tunnels? It has no claws."

The monster was quite clearly awake, and it hissed loudly as it reared up. Then the mouth opened. Because of her magic, Helaine felt a clear sense of danger and she yelled a warning to Rothar as she threw herself aside.

The wyrm spat a short stream of a luminous orange liquid from between its teeth. Thankfully, it missed them both, and hissed against the walls of the cave. Wherever the liquid hit, the rock seethed and burned, vaporizing.

"Acid," she breathed, shaken. "That's how it cuts the tunnels! It can spit acid! Rothar, stay away from that thing's mouth!"

"Believe me, I shall!" he agreed fervently. Drawing back his spear, he cast it at the wyrm as it reared up to release its poison again. The throw was good, but the wyrm shot another stream of acid out, catching the weapon and melting it before it could strike.

Refusing to be daunted, even though she was scared, Helaine rushed forward, under the upraised head, and slashed out with her sword. It cut into the wyrm's flesh, and the monster screamed and thrashed in pain. Helaine was showered in thin, smelly blood. And in the slime that the wyrm's tail was covered in. It was like taking a shower in glue. The liquid rained down on her before she could move, and she was covered quickly. Grimacing, she tried to back away.

And couldn't.

The slime didn't simply *feel* like glue, it acted like it, too. Horrified, Helaine realized that she was stuck in position, and unable to move more than a few inches as the slime started to solidify over her. "Rothar!" she gasped. "The thing's secreting some kind of glue. I can't move."

"Then I shall free you," Rothar replied, trying to move to her aid around the bulk of the wyrm. The wyrm seemed to have anticipated this, and blocked his path with its tail. Helaine could barely turn her head to see the action, but she could make out that the wyrm was emitting more of the slime. It was dripping from the creature onto the floor.

Rothar's heels were caught in it, and he gave a cry as he realized that he, too, was trapped. Quickly, he snatched up his bow and an arrow, aimed, and fired.

The arrow was too small a target for the wyrm to zero in on it properly. A stream of acid spit missed it completely, and the arrow buried itself in the creature's face, just below one of the red eyes. The wyrm gave a scream of pain, and slammed out with its tail. Unable to move his feet, all Rothar could do was duck.

The blow almost missed him, but not quite. Helaine flinched at the sound of the slap he received, and saw that it had stunned the centaur. It had also left him enveloped in the gluelike slime. They were both trapped now, and the wyrm knew it. It lowered its head, weaving from side to side, and then opened its huge mouth again.

Helaine winced as the massive head moved down toward the trapped centaur, who was struggling to regain his wits. He was absolutely defenseless now, and the wyrm obviously aimed to devour him. She couldn't let that happen! But what could she do? She couldn't move from the spot, and couldn't even throw her sword, even though it was free of the slime.

She had to use her magic, there was no other option. But what could she do? She couldn't throw a fireball, since she couldn't move her hands. Levitation? That wouldn't work. She could lift the wyrm without a problem, but it was too close to the roof of the nest already, so lifting it up a couple of feet wouldn't help. Helaine felt helpless, scared, and frustrated as the wyrm drew closer to its victim.

And then she realized she wasn't thinking properly again. There *was* something she could do. Maybe she couldn't levitate the wyrm, but there were other things she *could* levitate. She concentrated on the arrows in Rothar's quiver, and launched all eight remaining arrows as hard as she could in the wyrm's direction. Most of them slammed into the creature's face, and it howled in pain, anger, and confusion. It had been certain its victims were helpless, and now it *hurt*! It reared away from Rothar, who was now aware of what was happening. Furiously, he struggled to try to free himself, but couldn't manage it. The wyrm reared back, and Helaine realized that it was preparing to spit acid at the helpless centaur, thinking *he* had somehow caused the arrows to fire.

There was no more time now. Helaine grabbed her sword with the power of her sapphire, and lifted it up and then threw it as hard as she could manage against the wyrm. It buried itself up to the hilt just beneath one of the eyes.

For a second, nothing happened, and Helaine felt certain she'd failed. Then, almost slowly, the wyrm collapsed, thin, stinky blood and liquids gushing forth from the sword wound. The thing was dead.

Rothar gave a huge sigh of relief. "Well, you managed to kill it," he said, almost kindly. "Thank you for saving my life."

"You're welcome." Helaine was shaking with strain and relief. The monster was dead, and their troubles almost over.

"But we're still in something of a sticky situation," Rothar added. "I can't get free at all, and this stuff is getting harder all the time."

"I've got an idea," Helaine told him, thinking furiously. She reached out again with her mind, this time to the wyrm's mouth. There was a big pool of spit in there that the wyrm had been intending to fire at Rothar. Carefully, she levitated a couple of handfuls of the acid and brought it close to her. Drop by drop, she dripped it from the air onto the glop that held her fast to the floor. The acid seethed and hissed, but it was burning away the glue. In a couple of moments, her feet were free, and she could move away from the spot. She wasn't going to use the stuff on her body, of course. It would burn her in seconds. But on the floor, it was safe. She used the acid to free Rothar, and then dumped the rest of it on the floor, where it bubbled and seethed.

"You look ridiculous," Rothar informed her.

Helaine knew he was right — her hands were frozen into one position thanks to the glue, and she couldn't do a thing about it. And her hair had set like concrete into one shape. But Rothar looked no better.

"So do you," she informed him. "I could try to free you with an acid bath. . . ."

"Thank you, no," Rothar said with dignity. "I think I'd sooner wait and see if the goblins have some soap that might be effective." He stared at the wyrm's corpse in distaste. "I think it might be a good idea to start back now."

"I agree." Helaine used her levitation to jerk her sword free of the body, and cleaned it as best she could before floating it back to her scabbard.

CHAPTER 12

Pixel was glad to see Helaine. All the glue was gone, and her hair was wet but free again. Her clothes had been cleaned, and she'd obviously spent some time polishing her sword. "That's more like it," he commented enthusiastically.

"Well, I feel a lot better," Helaine agreed, shaking out her long blond hair. "That stuff was really disgusting."

Rothar, too, emerged cleaned and groomed. To Pixel's surprise, he even managed a smile in Helaine's direction. "I'm still not fond of humans," he informed her, "but you're certainly the best of a bad bunch. I almost like you."

"Careful," Helaine warned him. "People will begin to suspect you're actually nice."

Gunther clapped his hands together happily. Since Helaine and Rothar had returned and informed the goblins that the wyrm was dead, the goblin warrens had been filled with laughter and off-color goblin songs. "Right," Gunther announced, "there's no doubt at all that you've earned your reward. So follow me, all of you."

Pixel, Score, Helaine, Rothar, Dethrin, and Amaris dutifully followed behind him as the goblin leader took them through several long tunnels and then drew up in front of two large, barred doors. There were six goblins on duty there, all armed to the teeth. At a nod from Gunther, though, they scrambled to unbar and open the doors. All of them were grinning happily. They'd obviously heard the news.

"Take your pick of what you want," Gunther said, waving them inside.

Pixel wandered in and stopped in astonishment. The room was about a hundred feet deep, and at least fifty wide and high. It was piled high with treasures. There were gemstones of all shapes and colors, from beryls to diamonds, all glittering in the lights of the torches that the adventurers carried. There were stacks of gold and silver ingots, and other metals. The whole room had to be worth several fortunes — and not small ones, either. Pixel didn't know where to look first. It took his breath away.

Beside him, Amaris said in a hushed voice, "Sparklies. . . ."

Score swallowed. "Well," he said, his voice squeaking slightly, "I think we might be able to find a few things we can use here."

"I'll say," Helaine agreed. "Okay, let's look for the gems we need from our list." She took out the Book of Magic. "Jasper, agate, onyx, carnelian, chrysolite, beryl, topaz, chrysoprase, and jacinth."

"I don't even know what most of those look like," Pixel confessed.

"No problem," Gunther answered. "I know them all. Hang on." He burrowed into the pile of gemstones like a mole and, every now and then, a large jewel would come flying out. Each managed to catch one, and they ended up with three more gems apiece.

"That's enough," Helaine called, and Gunther reappeared, jewels showering off him as he emerged.

"That's all you want?" he asked. "I told you, you can take as much as you like."

Pixel shook his head even as he saw Score looking longingly at the treasure trove. "We need these gems to help us with our magic," he explained. "We really aren't trying to get rich off you. Besides, we'd have trouble carrying a fortune in gems while we're traveling and continually getting into trouble."

Nodding, Gunther turned to the centaurs. "You, too, are welcome to whatever you desire."

Amaris grinned and grabbed a double handful of jewels. "Thanks," she said happily, stuffing them into a shoulder bag she'd been given. "I can make a lot of jewelry with this stuff."

Rothar and Dethrin both took several jewels, slipping them into their packs. "That's enough," Rothar said. "We are not greedy creatures."

Gunther shrugged, looking puzzled. "Well, you're easy to reward, anyway," he commented. "Now for the other part of our bargain. I'll show you how to get to Shanara's palace. Follow me."

Pixel was excited as he followed along behind the goblin leader. The three new jewels he had in his pockets seemed to be burning into his soul. There was something very strange about having them. It seemed to be so *right*, as if he'd actually been sick all his life without knowing it, and now suddenly he was well again. He felt so alive, so filled with potential. He could almost feel the power within him growing at the touch of the gemstones. He remembered the recurring dream he'd been having, of a giant wheel of gemstones spinning. It seemed as if jewels had a great importance for him for some reason. As soon as he had the chance, he had to discover how to use these new jewels. Glancing at Helaine and then Score, he could see that they felt exactly the same way. There was a spring in their steps, despite the fact that they were now on their way to a showdown with the wizard Shanara.

She had tried to stop them several times, and she would undoubtedly do so again. Pixel was worried, and more than a little scared at the thought. She was much stronger than Aranak had ever been, and Aranak had almost killed them. Still, they had learned a lot since then. They weren't so raw and innocent as they had been. But had they learned enough to be able to face Shanara and live? Besides, maybe one of them was already Shanara. If so, she certainly knew that they were on their way, and would be able to lay a trap for them. It was impossible not to feel paranoid and uneasy. Was she with them? Was she setting a trap in motion? And could they possibly beat her?

Well, they'd soon find out. The thought deflated some of Pixel's new-found energy, and, as they walked the passageways, his spirits sank more and more.

Amaris obviously sensed this. She trotted to his side, and fell into step with him. "It's not too late," she told him. "You can always back out of this. You don't really have to face Shanara, do you? You could stay with the goblins. I'm sure they'd be happy to have you."

"It wouldn't work," said Pixel miserably. "There's still the Shadows. They helped us for their own reasons last time we met. But if we don't go on, they'll come after us. And if the goblins are in the way, they'll just kill the goblins. We can't do that to them. We have to go somewhere where nobody else can get hurt."

"Then prepare a weapon against Shanara," Amaris urged. "Don't let her get in the first shot. She might kill you if she has that advantage."

"Maybe," Pixel agreed. "But I can't do it. I'll defend myself if I have to, but I won't attack first, no matter how good the cause. It would make me no better than her, and I won't sink that low."

Amaris sighed and shook her head. "Stubborn," she said, "And very, very foolish. You may well be killed."

"True," admitted Pixel. "But I can't change what I am."

"No," agreed Amaris, somewhat wistfully. "The three of you are very nice people. It's a shame this isn't a nice world we're living in, where you would get what you deserve."

The tunnels led them upward, and they moved mostly in silence. Helaine and Score seemed to be as glum as Pixel felt, and probably for the same reason. None of them was looking forward to the upcoming fight, but what other option did they have? Shanara was their only way off this world, and they had to take the chance of confronting her. Otherwise they were either stuck here, or else their unknown foe would move them to where he, she, or it wanted them to go.

Pixel suddenly realized that he recognized the passageway they were in. At first he thought he had to be wrong, but then, as it opened out into a cave, he knew he wasn't mistaken. "It's the cave where the goblins attacked us!" he exclaimed, surprised.

"That's right," Helaine agreed. "This is where we first emerged onto this world!"

"Really?" Gunther shrugged. "Small world, eh? Well, we're close to the palace now." He led the way outside, and pointed up the mountain.

Pixel stared in amazement. At the top of the peak sat Shanara's palace. It looked as if it had been constructed out of blocks of ice, all shaped into the form of a large castle, with spires, turrets, and ramparts. It sparkled beautifully in the midday sun.

"It was above us all of the time!" groaned Score. "We didn't see it because it was covered in the clouds last time."

"Everything we went through these last few days was for nothing," complained Pixel.

"Not for nothing," Helaine contradicted. "We have the jewels now, and we've made some good friends. It was worth it for that. Still," she admitted, honestly, "I could kick myself anyway."

Pixel nodded. To have missed it by so little! It was bitterly cold, but the goblins had brought along fur cloaks for them, which they hastily donned. Gunther held up his hand.

"This is as far as we go," he said. "It's much too bright for us now. Besides, we don't bother Shanara, and she doesn't bother us. I don't want to get turned into a toad or anything." He smiled at Pixel and the others. "Good luck, allies. And if you come back this way, you will always be welcome with the goblins."

"Thanks," said Pixel. "For everything." Score and Helaine echoed his thanks.

With a final nod, Gunther and his men vanished back into the darkness of the cave. Pixel turned to look again at the magnificent castle. "Well," he said, "how do we get in?"

"Mgc," answered Helaine, holding her sapphire. "Hld nt yr stmchs."

Then they were all gripped by her levitation power, and flew off the ground and over the castle wall. Inside, there was a courtyard and a large door leading to the castle proper. It flew open as they approached, and they landed gently on the stone floor beyond. Only the outside of the castle was made of ice. Inside, it was quite cozy and stone-lined. Bright fires burned in huge fireplaces. There were trinkets, paintings, costly furniture, and drapes all over.

Using his ruby, Pixel found the room where the Page he was after lay. There was no sign of life in the castle at all. "Maybe she's not home?" he said hopefully.

"According to Oracle, she's one of us," Score replied. "So she's home *now*."

Pixel studied his five companions again as he led them up the huge stone staircase to the next floor. Was it true? Was one of them really Shanara in disguise? If so, who? And what was she waiting for?

"This is it," Pixel said, pushing open the door to Shanara's study. Inside lay the room he had seen in his vision earlier. There was a large desk, overflowing with books and papers. Down the center of the room was a long table filled with odd apparatus, and bottles and boxes of chemicals and other ingredients. Huge bookcases lined the walls. At the end of the room was a huge cauldron, filled with water.

And on a table beside the door lay the next Page. He knew it instantly, and snatched it up. As always, there was very little on it that made sense.

"Um, isn't it asking for trouble taking something that belongs to a wizard?" asked Rothar cautiously.

"It's not hers," Pixel said firmly. "It's *ours*. She was just safekeeping it. Or trying to steal it. But it's our property."

There was a sudden movement at the far end of the table. There was some kind of cat bed there, and a creature yawned, stretched, and said, in a very clear voice: "Back already, Shanara? I hadn't finished my nap yet and — uh-oh. . . ." The red panda sat up and stared at the party in shock. "What are *you* doing here?"

"That's her familiar!" Amaris exclaimed. "She uses it to enhance her own magic, like you use crystals! He can do magic himself."

"Then we'd better stop him," snapped Helaine. Using her gem, she lifted the panda off the bed and started to spin it around in the air.

"Hey!" it yelled, angry and obviously a little nauseous. "Stop that! I just ate! Put me down! Shanara, stop them!"

"So she *is* here!" Score said, triumphantly. "Okay, tell us who she is!"

"Ooooh!" the panda squealed. "Help! Shanara, I'm getting sick! Do something!"

Amaris was laughing so hard that tears were rolling down her face. "It's your own fault, Blink," she replied. "You're just too lazy. If you'd stayed on guard, like I told you, this would never have happened." She gestured, and the red panda's flight stopped, and he settled back into his bed. He looked very ill.

"You're Shanara!" Pixel exclaimed, jumping back from her instantly.

"That's right," she agreed. The shape of Amaris simply faded away, and was replaced by the form of a tall, beautiful, dark-haired woman in a long, warm dress. "I am."

Score fell into a defensive pose, and eyed her very suspiciously. "So — now we fight?"

"Fight?" Shanara laughed, and her eyes seemed to burn. Her form flowed again, becoming that of a sabre-toothed tiger. She threw back her head and roared. Instantly, she shifted again, this time into a horse-sized purple dragon, with long, nasty talons, and wings. Her mouth opened and she belched out a fireball that skimmed past them. Then she morphed again, this time into some kind of dinosaur, with a long, tooth-filled snout and razor-sharp claws. Then she returned to her human form. "Do you *really* think you can fight *me*?"

"Maybe not," Pixel agreed realistically. "But do we have a choice?" He swallowed, nervously trying to prepare himself for anything she might change into next. But that could literally be anything, and she would certainly pick something very lethal.

Shanara shrugged. "There's always a choice."

She crossed the room and picked up Blink. "I hope you learned a lesson from that," she scolded him.

"Are you going to fight?" asked Helaine, puzzled.

"Not unless you want to." Shanara stroked Blink and smiled cheerfully at their confused faces.

"I don't get it," Helaine said. "What do you want from us?"

"I want to help you on your way," Shanara said. "I can see you're very puzzled, so I think I'd better explain a few things. First of all, I detected you when you crossed into Rawn several days ago. I discovered that you'd killed Aranak, and that you were coming after me next. I assumed that you were evil, because most magicians tend to be, and you *had* killed Aranak. I tried to stop you, using the trolls. Then I realized that you had tried hard not to hurt them, and I wondered if I'd made a mistake about you. So I decided that I'd have to check you out in person, and I adopted the form of Amaris to do it."

Rothar turned to Dethrin with a scowl. "And you couldn't even tell it wasn't your sister?" he scoffed.

"Oh, I knew who she was all along," Dethrin said with a grin. "She often comes among us as Amaris."

Rothar's scowl darkened. "You *knew* and said nothing? Why?"

"Because of people like you," Shanara answered cheerfully. "Most centaurs don't like humans — and for pretty good reason. But I hate being on my own, and love to socialize. So I often visit your people in disguise. It's fun."

Pixel shook his head. "So you're not really evil?" he asked. "And there wasn't any danger that you'd kill us? Then why did you keep telling us that Shanara would, and urge us to attack her first?"

"Because I wanted to be certain you weren't just trying to trick me," the wizard explained, stroking Blink. He was almost purring like a cat. "I had to give you every opportunity to show your true colors. Which you did. You refused to steal from the goblins, and when they attacked you, you helped them. I'm glad we're not enemies."

"And to prove my good faith . . ." Shanara went to a bookcase and brought out a sheet of paper. "Here's the Page you were looking for."

Score took it eagerly, and held it as his friends studied it over his shoulders. "Well, it's as puzzling as ever," he said. "Still, there's that three at the top. That has to be either us or the Triad. And that *mirror, mirror* bit sounds as if Oracle had written it."

Pixel pointed to the three circles. "Treen, Rawn, and Dondar," he said. "We were on Treen, and this is Rawn, so the next world we're supposed to go to must be Dondar. The rest . . ." He shrugged.

"I'm sure you'll make sense of it when you have

THM ORACLM IS
NOT / RMAL

LISTMN

3

GIVE UP
THE GHOST GHOST

TREEN — RAHN — DONDAR — TRUTH

BEWARE
THEIR
——
KEEPER

This is how the mighty fall.

Mirror Mirror on the wall. This is how the mighty fall.

eet   the   future with the past. We are

dem   will fall. Come to us. In magic, w

the rest of the pages," Shanara said. "You're very bright, after all."

Pixel grinned. "So — now what?"

Shanara became all business. "I send you on your way," she replied. "I'll open the doorway you need into the next world, and you can cross through. Only . . ." She studied them for a moment. "We need to talk about where you're going."

Score snorted. "I don't care where we go," he replied, "as long as it's not Dondar. I just want out of this whole dumb business, to somewhere we can relax."

"Are you sure?" Shanara asked. "If you really want that, I can do it. But I don't think that's a very good idea."

"Why not?" demanded Pixel. "We're just sick and tired of all this fighting. We want some peace. Is that too much to ask? We never asked to be part of whatever's going on. We never asked to be magicians."

"Maybe not," agreed Shanara. "But, nevertheless, you *are* a part of it, and you *are* magicians. And potentially very powerful ones at that. You have more raw power than I've ever seen in magic-users. Way more than I have. Perhaps as much as the Three Who Rule. Because of that, you'll never be left in peace. I don't know who your foe is, but whoever it is wants you for some reason and won't stop looking for you."

"So?" asked Score. "We can hide out, and get stronger, then."

"Perhaps." Shanara looked at them very earnestly. "What I told you earlier about the Three Who Rule is true. They are the ultimate power in the Diadem, and they are corrupt tyrants. I think you are being trained as weapons against these tyrants. Perhaps you are being helped by the forces of good. Perhaps by someone who wishes to take their place himself. But I do know this — only you possess the power that might be able to defeat the Three. If you don't do it, they will continue their corrupt rule, and make life a misery for everyone throughout the Diadem."

Pixel finally understood what she was saying. "You want us to go up against them anyway?" he asked. "You're asking us to continue on the course that's been plotted out for us? To carry on the battle."

"Yes," Shanara agreed. "You're the only hope the Diadem has to be freed from tyranny and corruption. So I'm begging you — follow through, help everyone who dwells in the Diadem. Find the Three, defeat them and take their places. Free the Diadem from their evil rule." She studied their faces. "The one you call Oracle I have met once before. He bore a message from the Three Who Rule, so I assume that he is one of their servants. But who can tell where his true allegiance lies?"

Helaine sighed. "And the person who is sending the Shadows after us. Is that the Three?"

"No. The Shadows are a new force, and they are controlled by some hidden master. It may be that this master is one of the Three who fights the other two for sole power, or it may be some outsider. I do not know. But I do know this person will never stop hunting for you."

"Great," Pixel muttered. "All we want is a quiet life, and we're being co-opted into a war that we would rather not fight."

Helaine nodded. "But we're the only hope the Diadem has," she sighed. "Can we just turn our backs on them when we're needed?"

"Yes!" Score insisted. "It's not our problem. I'm sick of fighting. I just want some peace and quiet. We've done enough already. We freed the Beastials from Aranak, and we helped the goblins with that wyrm. We don't owe anybody else anything."

"True," agreed Shanara. "You have done your share. But . . . you have the power to do more. People need you. Centaurs, fauns, and all sorts of other creatures need you. Can you just walk away now and wash your hands of the whole thing?"

"Yes," Score insisted, but even to Pixel's ears he didn't sound certain. "I don't want to do it! I'm a coward, a liar, and a thief," he said. "Saving worlds really isn't my style."

Helaine sighed again. "But . . ."

"Don't start!" pleaded Score. "Come on, stand firm. We've got a chance to get out of it."

"I can't do it," Pixel confessed. "I know we'll be going into danger, and maybe facing getting killed again. But I can't just back out and pretend it's nothing to do with me. We're the only ones who stand a chance of freeing the Diadem."

"I don't care!" Score complained. "It's not our fault. I just want peace and quiet. Give me one good reason why I should agree to go with you."

"You've heard nothing but good reasons," said Helaine, a faint smile on her lips. "But if they don't convince you, I'll give you another. If you don't go with us, I'll cut your heart out." She tapped the hilt of her sword. "And you know I can do it."

"You wouldn't dare," snapped Score. But he didn't look completely convinced of that.

"Want to bet?" asked Helaine, raising an eyebrow. "Either that . . . or I'll kiss you."

Score shuddered. "I don't know which is worse." Then he shook his head and laughed. "I don't believe you'd do either, to be honest. But . . . okay, I give in. I'll go with you. But if I get killed, I promise I'm coming back to haunt the lot of you."

"You're already doing that," Helaine said drily.

Pixel turned back to Shanara. "Well, I guess we've made up our minds. Much as I hate the thought, we'll do what you ask. We'll take on the Three Who Rule, and either free the Diadem or else die trying."

"You are noble souls," Shanara said, approvingly. "Right, Blink — get your lazy hide to work. We need a gateway."

"Work, work, work," grumbled the panda. "Oh, very well, if it'll shut you up."

Dethrin stepped forward. "Thank you all," he said, sincerely. "I am proud to know you. You may always call me your friend." He clasped each of their hands in turn.

Rothar moved forward next, looking very uncomfortable. "I don't like humans," he growled. "But . . . you're not like any humans I've ever met before. I suppose you can call me your friend, too. Just don't do it when there are other centaurs around, okay?"

"Okay," agreed Helaine, laughing, and clasping his hand. "You're a real warrior, Rothar. I'm proud to have fought with you."

"This sentimental stuff always makes me sick,"

complained Blink, who looked around. "Okay, shape up. It's ready."

There was a familiar gash in space at the end of the room. Shanara's face was taut with concentration. "I can't hold it long," she said. "Hurry through — and may all good fortunes smile upon you."

Pixel screwed up all of his courage. He didn't like what they were doing much, but what other choice did they really have? Then he stepped into the gateway, and through to the new world beyond. . . .

EPILOGUE

The Shadows writhed and seethed about their master as he sat on his diamond throne, surveying the scene in a mirror. Stroking his beard, he laughed.

"The fools," he exclaimed. "Thinking that they can take on the Three Who Rule! Well, they still have a lot to learn. And they may just have the time to do so — before I destroy them." He shook his head. "They have no idea what is yet in store for them at all."

Standing up, the master surveyed the hundreds of Shadows who awaited his bidding. "I, Sarman, your master, am almost ready for the great stroke that will bring all of the Diadem under my rule. And those three idiots will provide me with precisely the power that I need. Very, very soon, there will no longer be Three Who Rule, but only One who rules supreme throughout the Diadem — Sarman!"

Shadowy laughter erupted all about the room as they contemplated his plan. Soon, very soon now, all would be over. . . .

ABOUT THE AUTHOR

JOHN PEEL is the author of numerous best-selling novels for young adults, including installments in the Star Trek, Are You Afraid of the Dark?, and Where in the World Is Carmen Sandiego? series. He is also the author of many acclaimed novels of science fiction, horror, and suspense.

Mr. Peel currently lives on the outer rim of the Diadem, on the planet popularly known as Earth.